The Widow

A Starlight Café Novel

by

Lovelyn Bettison

This is a work of fiction. Names and incidents are products of the author's imagination. Any resemblance to actual persons living or dead is entirely coincidental.

Nebulous Mooch Publishing

2018

Chapter One

BETTY flung her arms up and laughed. Her pale blue eyes gleamed with the thrill of victory. "Didn't I tell you we would win?" She threw her cards on the table with a slap before adjusting her perfectly coifed lemon-yellow bob.

The Starlight Café teemed with life. The lunchtime crowd poured in, filling the tables. Men and women gathered together in clusters, sipping on caffeinated beverages and talking loudly. At other tables, people sat quietly, reading books or doing work on their computers. Even though this place was almost always full, Connie, the owner, never had a problem with Betty and her friends playing cards there once a week.

"We always make a great team." Pat tugged at her lilac T-shirt.

"I swear you two cheat," Dorothy grumbled, patting her recently dyed hair. The unnatural-looking red, nestled atop her head, looked like a toxic cloud.

"How dare you accuse us of cheating?" Betty laughed. "It's not my fault you're bad at the game."

"We've been friends so long that we have a special

connection." Pat gathered up the cards.

Lydia scowled. "A cheating connection." She cocked her head and looked at Dorothy knowingly. Her long gray hair was pulled up into a neat bun. She wore a black knit shirt with a pair of gray wide-leg linen pants. At seventy-two, she was the youngest of the group. Her sharp, stern face contrasted her bubbly personality. She glanced down at the gold chain watch she wore on her wrist. "This has been fun as usual, ladies, but I have an appointment to get to."

"Lydia's always so busy." Dorothy passed her cards to Pat.

"That's right, I am. I can't sit around all day. I'd go crazy." Lydia stood.

"Who are you accusing of sitting around all day?" Dorothy asked.

"I'm guilty." Pat waved her hand in the air like an enthusiastic grade-school student. "After forty years of teaching school, I think I've earned the right."

Lydia looked at her watch again. "It's been fun, but I have an important date."

"A date?" Betty raised an eyebrow.

"Oooh," Betty, Pat, and Dorothy said together.

"Why are you keeping this a secret?" Dorothy poked Lydia's arm.

"If it was secret, I wouldn't have told you just now." Lydia retrieved her handbag from the back of her chair and looped it into the crook of her elbow.

"Who is it?" Pat always got straight to the point.

"Nobody you know. He doesn't live in the building." Lydia looked up at the entrance. "I really have to go. I'm running late." She started walking away from the table and then turned around. "See you ladies later."

"You better have some news for me about your date later," Dorothy called after her.

Lydia hurried away on long, slender legs.

The ladies sat quietly for a moment, listening to the buzz of the coffee shop and smelling the earthy aroma of freshly brewed coffee.

"How is Bernie doing these days?" Betty asked Pat.

Pat sighed. "Some days are better than others. I still don't know if I made the right decision when I decided to put him in the nursing home."

Alzheimer's disease was eating away at Bernie's brain. Even though he was still in the early stages, he'd gotten to be too difficult for Pat. At first, it was just forgetfulness. Pat was around most of the time and could manage it, but when he started forgetting her, it got to be too much. Confused and agitated, he would become violent. She had to call an ambulance more than once, and the final time, the social worker suggested she put him in continuous care. "I feel like I failed him. When we got married, we promised to take care of each other."

"That's what you're doing. You couldn't have taken care of him on your own. They can do it better than you," Dorothy reassured. "You made the best decision for both of you."

"Every time I visit him, I think about all the time I wasted. I wish we'd done more together. We saved money and invested well. We prepared for just about anything, but we were both always healthy. We assumed we'd spend this time traveling." She reached over and picked up the deck of cards. "I wish I could go back in time and start again."

"What would you do differently?" Betty was curious. She couldn't help but think about all her own regrets. Her husband, Sam, had died so suddenly. Once he was gone, she found herself wishing they had had more time together.

"I would've taken the trips we wanted to take sooner. We

were always putting things off. It's a bad habit to have. Now it's too late."

"You had no way of predicting the future. None of us do," Betty said.

Pat shrugged. "I know, but that's what I've been thinking about." She rapped the cards on the table. "Some days he's fine. It's like nothing is wrong with him at all. I cherish those days. I know they'll be fewer and further between as he progresses."

"Cherish the moments you have now. That's all you can do," Dorothy said.

"That's what I keep telling myself."

Dorothy gave Pat's hand a squeeze before turning her attention to Betty. "We miss you in the building."

"I miss living in the building." Betty loved living with her family, but sometimes she longed for the privacy of her old studio apartment.

"The place isn't the same without you." Pat put the deck of cards into the box and stuck them in her red quilted purse.

"You'll be back in no time." Dorothy always said that, but Betty and everyone else knew she was never going to move back.

"I think I'm at Ethan's to stay. My last fall was pretty serious." Her broken ribs still hadn't healed completely. She hated giving up her independence, but she kept trying to tell herself that this was better. Ethan was right. It was safer, and she got to live with her granddaughters, Imani and Maia.

"You're lucky your family is right here," Dorothy said. "If any of my children decided I had to live with them, I'd have to go up north to the cold. I certainly wouldn't be ready to do that, but I do wish my grandchildren were closer."

Betty tried to remind herself how lucky she was all the time.

"Do you ladies need anything?" Connie asked as she cleared the dirty coffee cups from the table next to theirs.

"We were all just leaving, but thank you for asking," Betty said. "How have you been, Connie?"

Connie stood with a stack of white cups in hand. "Very good. I was going through some pretty rough stuff for a little while there, but things are starting to come together now."

"Good to hear that," Dorothy said.

"Nice seeing you ladies, as always." Connie went back over to the counter, balancing her stack of cups.

"On that note, we should go too." Dorothy stood, and Pat followed her lead. "Is your daughter-in-law coming to pick you up?"

"She should be here any minute." Betty looked at the clock on the wall. Tawana was always on time.

"We can wait here until she shows up." Pat twisted around and looked at the clock on the wall behind them.

"Don't worry about it. You two should get going."

"Are you trying to get rid of us?" Dorothy asked.

Before Betty could answer, her daughter-in-law walked through the door. Her confident stride made her the center of attention wherever she went. Her black hair was slicked up into a short ponytail. Her dark brown skin was flawless. Her long, flowing skirt danced around her legs as she walked. Somehow, she always managed to look immaculate despite the Florida heat and her two active daughters, nine-year-old Imani and six-year-old Maia.

"Grandma!" Maia ran across the coffee shop, nearly bumping into a woman.

"Maia!" Tawana hollered after her. "Watch where you're going." She turned to the woman who'd almost dropped her coffee. "I'm sorry about that."

When Maia reached Betty, she threw her arms around her.

She smelled of sweat and strawberry candy. Her hair was neatly parted down the middle and plaited in two French braids that curled up at the ends. Maia was the perfect mashup of both her parents. She had Tawana's almond-shaped eyes and her father's small mouth. Her long, dark eyelashes curled so much that the tips nearly touched her upper lids.

Imani, the oldest of the two girls, inherited her father's straight nose and thin mouth. Her hazel eyes seemed to change color according to what she wore. Her black curls fell in large ringlets down her back.

When Ethan and Tawana first got married, Betty and Sam didn't know what to think. Part of them was happy he finally decided to marry, but they were also worried. Betty hated to admit it now, but she did have her misgivings. She never spoke them out loud to anyone but Sam. Looking at her granddaughters now made her realize how wrong she was to worry. She couldn't imagine not having Tawana and the girls in her life.

"How was the game?" Tawana sidled up to the table with Imani close behind her.

"It was great. We won." Pat pointed at Betty and back at herself.

"You were lucky this time," Dorothy said. "We'll get you two next week."

"Do you want to bet on that?" Pat asked.

"No betting," Betty said. They had made that rule when they first started playing. Wagers, no matter how playful, could sour friendships over time.

"It was nice seeing you again." Dorothy put a hand on Tawana's upper arm and smiled broadly. "We really should get going."

With that, the two ladies took off. Betty watched them go and waited until they were outside before she spoke. "Could you help me up, dear? My back is killing me. Honestly, I don't think I'm able to stand on my own." She took her cane in one hand, and Tawana pulled her up by the other. She swore she could hear her hips creak as she rose to her feet. She was a little unsteady. Tawana held onto her arm and looked into her eyes, not letting go until Betty gave the word, an almost imperceptible nod.

"Are you okay?" Tawana was one of the few people who knew how bad Betty's pain was.

"I'm just a little creaky today, but I'll be fine." Betty moved her silver cane forward and took a step. "See, no problem. Let's go to the car."

In the car on the way home, Tawana drove slowly, swinging the car wide around as many of the bumps in the road as she could. She was sure to take her time as she turned corners because she knew every jerk and bump hurt. Betty appreciated little things like that even though her appreciation went unspoken.

Maia chattered in the back seat about her day at the science museum.

"I want to go to the science museum too," Imani said after Maia had gone into great detail about the earthquake exhibit, she'd seen that day.

"We'll go together." Tawana looked in the rearview mirror at Imani's earnest face. "We didn't go for fun today. There was a homeschooling activity with the science group. You know that, Imani. It happens during school hours, and I'm not going to pull you out of school for it. We can go to the science museum one day when there is no school. That way we can have time to look at all the exhibits. Maia only got to see a few because she was there for another activity."

"When you take Imani, I want to go too," Maia chirped.

"Of course, we'll all go."

Imani crossed her arms and pouted. "I don't want her to go. You always spend time with her and not with me."

"I go places alone with Maia for school. We can go somewhere special, just the two of us this weekend, but it would be best for us all to go to the science museum together. Maybe Grandma would want to go too."

Betty shook her head. The idea of walking around the science museum didn't appeal to her. She loved spending time with the girls, but she was feeling particularly weak these days. "I don't know. It depends on how I feel."

"Of course." Tawana pulled the car up in front of their wooden two-story house. It had gotten a new coat of paint the previous week--steel blue. Betty still wasn't sure why Tawana had chosen the color. She liked the original sage green much better. Spanish moss swayed on the branches of the old oaks surrounding the house. It pleased Betty that her son was so successful that he could afford a nice house. She knew from experience that many of the homes in the area were much more expensive than anything she and Sam could've afforded.

Tawana helped her out of the car and up the front stairs. "I was going to make the girls snacks. Do you want anything?"

"I want a chocolate chip cookie," Maia said.

Imani was already headed upstairs, her hard-soled shoes smacking the wooden steps.

"Don't stomp," Tawana yelled.

Imani's footsteps quieted.

"I had a croissant already." Betty always got a croissant at the coffee shop. She couldn't resist the flaky, buttery pastry. "I don't feel much like eating right now."

"Okay, but remember a croissant isn't a meal."

"I want a croissant." Maia jumped up and down.

Tawana put her hand on her hip and looked down at the

child. "We don't have any croissants or chocolate chip cookies. You can have an oatmeal cookie or apple slices with peanut butter."

Maia stopped and stuck out her bottom lip. She left the kitchen and stomped up the stairs.

"Stop stomping!" Tawana yelled. She shook her head.

"I think I'll just lie down for a little bit." Betty felt woozy. These days, drinking coffee didn't do anything to wake her up. When she was younger, it made her excited in a fluttery way. "I'm feeling a bit tired."

Betty had the only bedroom downstairs. She took her time going down the hallway off the kitchen to her bedroom. She liked it there because it was like having her own little apartment tucked away from the rest of the house. She had her own bathroom and could wander into the kitchen anytime she wanted for a snack.

Once she got to her room, she ducked into the bathroom and took a painkiller. The chalky pill scratched her throat as it went down. She wished the pills worked instantly, but she had a whole twenty minutes before it would begin to take effect. She would probably be asleep by then.

Unlike the rest of the house, a lush beige carpet covered the floor in Betty's room. Ethan had it installed before she moved in because he thought it made her less likely to slip and fall. Her full-sized bed flanked the wall opposite the door. A pink and yellow flowered chair sat next to the window. Betty had decorated the room with family pictures in dollar-store frames.

She sat on the edge of the bed and took a few deep breaths. A dull ache gnawed at her lower ribs and hips. She slipped off her sandals and lay on top of the blanket, not even bothering to pull it back. Often when she was alone in her room, she swore she could feel someone else there with her.

When she closed her eyes, she could feel Sam lying beside her. She inhaled deeply, hoping to smell him, but she didn't. He'd died years ago, but it still felt like she'd been with him only yesterday. His loss was one wound that remained raw and sore no matter how much time had passed. She missed him every day. In those rare moments when the world was quiet around her, she sometimes thought she could hear him whispering in her ear. She thought of him before drifting off to sleep. She always did.

Betty intended to take a short nap. She loved naps these days. Sleep was the ideal escape. It was hard to believe that there was a time when, as a child, she would fight the idea of going to bed. Now she longed for sleep.

That afternoon when Betty lay down, she had no idea that her dreams would start to change, remaking her life into something entirely different.

Chapter Two

SAM walked because his car had broken down. It had been out of service for most of the week, leaving him dependent on rides from friends and his father, or alternatively, his own feet. There wasn't much use in getting the car fixed because he'd be leaving soon. He'd been drafted to fight a war on the other side of the world. Secretly he was scared, but he would never tell anyone that.

He was walking down Central Avenue when he saw the most exquisite girl he'd ever seen. She wore her caramel-colored hair in a single ponytail. She stood in front of the ice cream shop wearing a simple white blouse and navy-blue skirt as she concentrated on picking something from her hands. A taller, dark-haired girl stood next to her eating an ice cream cone and talking. As he approached them, Sam took the white handkerchief from his pocket and held it out to the girl.

"Maybe you could use this," he said.

She turned her heart-shaped face toward him, looking startled.

"I didn't mean to scare you. I was just offering a handkerchief." He waved the white piece of cloth in the air. Noticing she was still looking a bit baffled, he added, "It's clean. I swear I haven't used it."

The dark-haired girl laughed. "You should take it, Betty. You'll never get all of that off your hands."

Her name was Betty. Sam took a mental note. "Come on, Betty." He shook the handkerchief in the air one last time.

"I don't see how that'll help me. Thank you anyway." She looked around. "What I need is some water." She spun on her heels and ducked into the ice cream parlor.

Sam watched her through the glass door as she bounced through the shop. When he looked at her dark-haired companion, she was staring at him. "I'm Pat," the girl said. "Do you go to school with us? I swear I've seen you."

Sam shook his head and looked back at the doorway, hoping to see Betty again. "I graduated last year. My name's Sam."

Pat looked toward the door of the ice cream parlor and then back to Sam. "Don't worry, she's coming back."

Sam cleared his throat and put the handkerchief back in the pocket of his khaki pants. "I wasn't worried."

"Okay." She giggled again. "I should probably tell you that she already has a boyfriend. They've been going steady for five months. If you ask me, he might be the one."

Sam looked at Pat in disbelief. How silly of him to think that someone as lovely as Betty might be available. Still, he wanted to hear it from her.

He looked back to the ice cream shop and spotted Betty moving amongst the other patrons. She walked toward the door, hips swaying and a smile spread across her face. She pushed the door open with a flourish and, holding her hands up in front of her, said, "All clean." She looked right into Sam's eyes, her clear blue ones shining brightly. "Thanks for offering to help."

Sam shrugged and reached into his pocket, feeling the soft

fabric of the handkerchief. He wished she had used it.

"Sam here was just asking about your boyfriend, Tucker." Pat grinned devilishly before taking a bite of her ice cream cone.

"You know Tucker?" Betty smiled enthusiastically.

Sam shot Pat a sidelong glance before shaking his head. "Not exactly."

Betty tilted her head at him. "Did you want to know something about him?"

"It wasn't important." He scowled at Pat. "I'm going to get an ice cream cone. Do you want another one?" he asked Betty.

"No, thank you. One is enough for me. I don't want to spend the night with a stomachache."

By the time he got out of the ice cream parlor with his chocolate cone in hand, Betty and Pat were gone. He looked up the street and thought he caught a glimpse of them a few blocks away. He jogged after them. When he caught up, he was winded. Sweat ran down his face. "I can't believe you left me."

They both looked at him in shock. He had to stop startling them; it was no way to win a girl over.

"I didn't know we were supposed to wait for you," Betty said.

"Last time I checked, we weren't together," Pat said. They walked at a steady clip, neither of them slowing down to talk to him. His ice cream had begun to melt. Cold, sticky liquid ran down his hand. He bit off the ice cream, taking it down almost all the way to the cone.

Noticing, Pat said, "You have a big mouth."

Sam flushed with embarrassment. "It's melting. I have to eat it fast."

"See, Betty. He understands that you shouldn't let your ice

cream melt all of your hands while you talk nonstop."

"You were the one doing all the talking. I was listening." Betty looked straight ahead while she spoke.

"The secret to not having a melting cone is getting it dipped in chocolate. The hard chocolate shell keeps the ice cream from melting on your hands."

"You know I'm not such a big fan of chocolate."

"Oh yeah. I forgot you're a weirdo."

"No, I'm not." They bantered back and forth like he wasn't even there. "There are tons of people who don't like chocolate."

"Where are you girls headed?" Sam wanted desperately to get back into the conversation.

"Just walking around. Wasting time, you know?" Pat said.

"What a coincidence. That's just what I'm doing." He took another giant bite of his ice cream, and his head started to hurt. He winced.

"You ate that fast." Betty turned and looked at him for the first time.

"I'm paying for it now." He tried to smile through the stabbing pain of his brain freeze.

"If I eat my ice cream too fast, I always get a headache." Betty's voice was like music.

"Ice cream headaches are the worst," he said, happy she was finally talking.

"So, you know Tucker?"

"No. I think I've heard of him though." Sam remembered a kid named Tucker in high school. "Does he play basketball?"

She nodded enthusiastically. "That's him. He's a terrific player, isn't he?"

"To be honest, I've never seen him play. I'm not too into sports."

"Not into sports?" Pat turned and looked at him with her

mouth agape. "What do you do, then?"

"This and that," Sam said, realizing it was a stupid answer. "I run."

"Why do you do that?" Pat asked.

"For fun and exercise."

"That's crazy. Who does that?" Pat screwed up her face. "He's as much of a weirdo as you." She poked Betty.

"Isn't that a sport?" Betty ignored Pat's weirdo comment.

"It is. I ran cross-country in school. It was the only athletic thing I was interested in. I'm more of a loner."

"So am I," Pat said. Somehow Sam didn't believe her.

"I'm not." Betty's thin, graceful arms swung when she walked, like she might break into a dance at any moment. "Being alone for too long makes me feel nervous."

"What about?" Sam couldn't imagine not liking to spend time alone. He found comfort in solitude.

Betty shrugged. "I'm not sure. I guess when I'm by myself, my mind gets all full. My thoughts start racing, and I feel like I might...." Betty sighed. "It's hard to explain."

"Some people don't like to spend time alone because they're afraid of what they'll find out about themselves." Sam never felt that way, but he'd read it somewhere.

"Listen to you getting all philosophical on us." Pat bumped him with her hip, throwing him off balance.

"I'm not trying to get philosophical." He paused for a moment. "When you're alone, it makes you start to think about who you are. For some people, that's scary because they're not sure yet. The paradoxical thing is that the only way to start to be sure of who you are and what you believe in is to spend some time alone thinking about it."

"Is that what you think about when you're running?" Betty turned to face him again. He liked it when she was looking at him.

"Yeah. I think about a lot of stuff like that. I don't run that much anymore. I just did that for school."

"Really? Maybe you should start running again. It'll give you time to think." Betty smirked when she said it.

"That would be a gas," Pat said. "Seeing you in your little shorts running around town for no reason at all."

"I'll be running again soon enough. I've been drafted for Korea. I report next week." Of all the dumb luck in the world, of course Sam would meet someone like Betty right before he was due to report for basic training. She was exactly the kind of girl he had been looking for all this time. He wanted to ask her where she'd been all his life, but she had a boyfriend. She'd made that clear already, and from what he remembered, Tucker was an okay guy--athletic, good-looking, and exactly what any girl was looking for. Thinking about him made Sam feel self-conscious about his lanky frame. He was all angles and sharp edges, and no matter how much he ate, he never put on weight.

"Seriously? Tucker is going to Korea next week too. You two will probably be in the same basic training." In her enthusiasm, she grabbed hold of his forearm with her soft, smooth hand. "That means you two could look out for each other. Tucker's being brave about it, but I'm scared for him, you know?"

"That's only natural." Sam was worried, but he knew he had to be brave. "I'll be sure to look out for him. You never know, we could end up in the same unit."

"This is so lucky. I can't wait to tell Tucker that I met someone he'll be serving with. It's silly, but it really does make me feel better."

"Are you scared to go off to war?" Pat asked.

"A little. My father says I'll be fine if I follow instructions and make sure I shoot them before they shoot me."

"If you do that, hopefully you'll be fine. I feel like anything could happen there." Betty looked straight ahead again. They turned to walk toward the neighborhood where houses sat at the front of small lots on tree-lined brick streets. "You're going this way too?" Betty asked.

"Just for a little way." Sam didn't know how long he should walk with them. He was wondering if it was getting to be a bit weird for them and considered going a different way.

They walked quietly for a little bit. Women sat outside on their porches, their rocking chairs creaking in the heat. Many waved and spoke as they went by, saying "Good afternoon" and "Isn't it a hot day?" Betty always had something to say back.

In between the greetings from the old ladies on the porches, Sam used their time together to find out everything he could about Betty. She said she loved living in Saint Petersburg and wanted to stay forever. Sam understood that feeling, but he wanted to travel the world. He imagined himself going on vacations in exotic places, eating food he'd never heard of before and wearing interesting clothing. He'd come back to tell all his friends about his experiences. He'd probably run the family sandwich shop when his father passed away, but he didn't want to think about that yet.

When they got to the corner of his street, he considered continuing to walk with them but decided he'd better not. "I go this way." He pointed down the side street.

Betty opened her purse and pulled out a pen and a scrap of paper. "We're having a going-away party for Tucker. It would be good if you came too. A bunch of kids from school are going."

Sam's heart danced in his chest. His cells felt like they would ignite. She was inviting him somewhere. Sure, it was to her boyfriend's party, but it was a start. He couldn't be too picky right now. "Okay. I'd like to go. Let me give you my phone number."

Betty used the hard surface of her purse to write on. She pressed the pen firmly into the paper as she scrolled out Sam's number. Her writing was large and loopy, just like Sam imagined it would be.

"I'll call you and let you know where and when it is." She held up the piece of paper and looked at the number as if trying to commit it to memory before sticking it into her bag. "You'll come, won't you?"

Sam thought it was crazy that she would even ask such a question. He would go wherever she asked him to go.

"Of course he will. He likes you," Pat said.

They both looked at her and back at each other. Uncomfortable silence floated in the air. Sam took a few seconds to recover before speaking again. "Yes, I'll go. Just call and let me know."

"Good." They stood looking down the street Sam's house was on. "Well, we're going this way." Betty pointed down the other street.

"It was nice meeting you, Betty and Pat. I can't wait to see you at the party."

Sam stood on the corner and watched them walk up the street before continuing down his own street. He had been invited to a party by one of the most beautiful girls he had ever seen. He couldn't wait to go. He hoped she'd remember to call him and tell him the details, but until then he had to be satisfied with the memory of her.

Chapter Three

THE sun was starting to go down when Betty opened her eyes. Dusty beams of light streamed through the cracks in the curtain. Betty's clothes were wrinkled from sleep. Her tongue felt thick and cottony. She looked at the red numbers on the clock on her bedside table. It was dinnertime. She hadn't meant to nap so long, but the dreams of Sam often kept her wrapped in sleep for hours. His memory lifted her spirits. In this dream, they were so young. His thick dark brown hair was cut close to his head. He still had the wiry frame of youth. She'd always remember the day they met. She'd liked him right away, even though she was hesitant to show it.

The smell of chili wafted into her room, making her stomach growl.

There was a knock at her door, followed by a timid voice. "Grandma, it's dinnertime." It was Imani.

"Come in." Betty's voice creaked. She leaned over and turned on the lamp, lighting up the room with the yellowish glow. Her room was simple. There was a full-size bed against the wall. Next to it, a small bookshelf displayed her collection of murder mysteries. All her clothes fit neatly into the large walk-in closet. Off to the side was a bathroom with a shower that was just right for her. Tawana had made sure to buy her a shower chair when she moved in. At the time, Betty insisted it wasn't necessary, but secretly, she was grateful to have it and used it every morning.

Imani pushed the door open and stepped inside. "Mommy told me to tell you dinner was ready." She walked up to the bed and stood directly in front of Betty.

"Could you give me a hug to help me wake up?" Betty held her arms open.

Imani reached up and held her tightly. She was a lot gentler than her sister. They hugged for a long time. There was something special about a hug from her granddaughter. The children made her tired sometimes, but knowing they were a part of her that would continue long after she passed on brought her more joy than she could even begin to explain.

Imani stepped away from her. She pulled at the hem of her T-shirt.

"Don't do that. You'll stretch your shirt out of shape," Betty said.

Imani stopped suddenly, looked up at her and nodded. "We're having chili. Mommy bought tortilla chips and salsa for us to eat too. I like salsa."

"So do I."

*

Betty often swore she could feel Sam close to her, even years after he'd passed away. She leaned heavily on her cane as she followed Imani into the kitchen. When her hips ached like this, she sometimes thought she could feel Sam holding her up.

Tawana ladled the chili into white bowls. Maia stood behind her, hands outstretched. "Can you take this to the table without dropping it?" Tawana said before putting the bowl of chili in her daughter's hand. "You too, Imani. Come get a bowl."

Imani took a bowl from the counter to her seat at the table.

Maia was much more careful with hers. She walked slowly, staring at her bowl the whole time.

Betty stood in the kitchen doorway looking around. "Is Ethan home?"

"He's working late again." Tawana's voice was flat.

"He always works late. I wish he would eat dinner with us sometimes," Betty said, voicing what she assumed everyone else was thinking.

"So do I, but what can I do?" Tawana shrugged. She pulled out her chair and sat down at the table. "Come on, girls. Let's eat."

Maia and Imani scrambled to their seats. They both grabbed a handful of tortilla chips from the bowl in the middle of the table.

"Don't eat more chips than chili," Tawana warned.

Neither of the girls responded. They noisily crunched on chips and acted like they didn't hear her.

Chili night was one of the few times Maia didn't talk at all through dinner because she was too busy eating.

The chili was thick and flavorful with just the right amount of spice. Tawana was an excellent cook. Betty had gained weight since moving in with them. She wasn't complaining. She was never much of a chef and had grown tired of frozen meals.

As she ate, Betty kept thinking about her dream. It was so clear that it was as if it had happened just yesterday.

Sam was the love of her life. He died so suddenly that it sucked the air out of her. Usually, if someone had cancer, you had time to prepare. Death came slowly, or at least that's what

Betty always thought until it happened to Sam. It was a rare kind that ate up his insides, pulling him away so quickly that there was almost no time to say goodbye.

What started as a steady ache in his back progressed quickly to him doubled over in pain and needing to go to the emergency room. His doctor's face telegraphed the bad news before she even spoke. They weren't prepared for how bad. Tumors riddled his insides. The doctor told them it was a miracle he had lasted as long as he had with so much disease inside of him.

Sam was strong and lucky. Nothing could stop him. That was why Betty had been so sure they could fight it. Even when everyone else thought it was impossible, she was confident that they could beat it. They had overcome a lot together: the death of a child, financial disaster, the death of their parents. They could overcome this too. She just knew it. Even when Sam stopped believing, she was still convinced, holding on to the idea that the doctors didn't know anything, and they could make it through.

Looking back, it was all because she didn't want to believe. She wanted them to be wrong. She was the person looking at the sky and insisting it was clear when everyone else saw storm clouds. She was convinced that if she believed it strongly enough, it would come true. God didn't agree with her.

Months after he died, she blamed him. She had all the faith, all the belief. He didn't believe strongly enough to make it happen. She'd hung on to that anger until her best friend, Pat, told her it was doing her no good. She had to let go, but letting go was hard. Losing Sam had broken her, but as she clawed her way back into the world, she remade herself into someone stronger than she'd ever been. The lessons learned didn't make up for losing her husband, but they were what made her.

"Are you okay?" Imani looked at her with round eyes as she stuck a heaping spoonful of chili into her mouth.

Betty realized she had been sitting holding her spoon in midair. Chili dripped off the edges into the bowl as she stared down at the table. She put her spoon in the bowl. "I was just daydreaming."

"You can't be daydreaming," Maia said. "It's dark outside."

"Technically, it's evening." Imani's words dripped with confidence.

"Should I say I was evening dreaming, then?" Betty smiled at the girls and waited for their answers.

"Maybe you're just dreaming." Imani's response was quick.

"What were you dreaming about?" Maia asked.

"Maybe your grandmother wants to eat in peace." Tawana absentmindedly scrolled through her phone at the table.

"It's fine. I welcome the questions," she said. "I was thinking about your grandfather and how much I miss him."

"Why?" Maia's mouth was smeared with chili.

"When someone's not here, you miss them. Remember when your mother went away a few months ago?"

"You cried," Imani taunted. "You're such a baby."

"Imani, be nice to your sister." Tawana turned her phone face down on the table and started to eat.

"I am not." Maia folded her arms.

"It's okay to cry when you miss someone. There's no shame in that," Betty said. "That's how I feel about your grandfather being gone."

Maia crinkled her forehead, her thread-thin eyebrows furrowed. "But he's not gone. He's right there." Everyone's eyes followed her finger as it pointed at the empty chair Ethan usually occupied.

"That's not funny," Tawana scolded.

"I know." Maia frowned and lowered her finger. "He's gone now. He said it's not polite to point." She picked up a chip and took a bite.

A chill scurried up Betty's spine.

"Maia." Tawana looked at the chair and then back at Maia. "Jokes like that aren't very nice for your grandmother."

Maia slid off the chair onto the floor. "It's not a joke. It's not. It's not," she wailed, showing the white specks of tortilla chips on her tongue.

"Great." Imani raised her shoulders in an exaggerated shrug and rolled her eyes. "Can't we just eat dinner in peace?" she said, mimicking her mother.

Maia's meltdown faded into the background as Betty stared at the empty straight-back chair sitting beside her. She sat next to that chair so often when it was empty. Could Sam really still be with her? Could this feeling she sometimes had be real?

It didn't take long for Tawana to calm Maia down and get her back in her chair. She had been much worse when Betty first moved in, but as time passed, her tantrums got shorter and shorter. With them all back at the table, the conversation continued as if nothing had happened.

"I never met Grandpa." Imani was so matter of fact.

"I did," Maia said, and Tawana gave her a stern look. "I--"

Tawana pointed her finger at her, and Maia stopped talking.

"I know you didn't, but I sure wish you had. He would've been so proud," Betty said. That made them smile.

"What was his favorite color?" Imani used a paper towel to wipe the chili from her chin.

"Green." Maia covered her mouth with both her hands, as if trying to keep more words from leaping out.

"That's right." Betty's heart thudded in her chest. "How

did you know that?" Her question was cautious.

"He told me." Maia's answer was just as cautious.

"Maia, enough!" Tawana shook her head in exasperation. "Just eat your dinner."

"Grandma asked," she whined.

"I did ask." Betty inhaled, trying to calm her racing heart. She'd wanted him back so badly. Seeing that continuing to question Maia would only upset Tawana, she decided against it. "He didn't care about the shade, just as long as it was green. I think that's why he was always so good with plants. We had the best-looking yard on the whole block and a great vegetable garden."

Maia stuck out her tongue. "Vegetables, yuck."

"If you were willing to try them, I'm sure you'd find some you like," Tawana said, looking up from her phone. "I loved all of the canna lilies you had in your front yard."

"What's a candle lily?" Imani asked.

"Canna," Betty said. "It's a tall colorful flower with big leaves." Betty could easily picture the plants clustered in the flower bed next to the front porch. They lived in that adorable little bungalow for most of their marriage. They didn't need that much space because they were a small family. Sam would spend hours out in the yard weeding and planting flowers. They always had fresh vegetables to eat. Sam would come inside with a bundle of greens and soil in the creases of his fingers and packed beneath his nails. The musty, damp scent of newly turned earth clung to his clothes. Sometimes Betty swore she could still smell him.

Tawana held up her phone to show the girls a picture of a canna lily, its canary-yellow bloom perched atop a tall stem.

"That's it?" Maia said.

"You sound disappointed," Betty said.

"No." Maia shook her head emphatically. "It's pretty. I

wanted it to be red."

Tawana turned the phone around and tapped it a few times. When she turned back around to show Maia the screen, there was a blood-red flower on it. "Is that better?"

Maia nodded.

*

The girls were in bed by the time Ethan came home. Betty was emptying the dishwasher in the kitchen. She'd sent Tawana to the living room to relax with a glass of wine. Betty heard the click of the door shutting over the noise of the television.

"You're late," Tawana said. There was no anger in her voice. She was too tired for that.

Ethan mumbled his answer. Betty didn't hear what he said. She stood with the plate in her hand next to the opened cabinet, listening. She wanted to make sure they weren't fighting before she came out. Hearing nothing, she put the plate in the cabinet and turned to walk into the living room when Ethan appeared at the doorway.

The first two buttons of his white shirt were undone, and his tie was loosened. His suit coat was slung over his arm, his dark hair tousled, his eyelids dropping over his sunken dark eyes. He looked like his father, if his father hadn't taken care of himself. Ethan never was much for exercise or spending time outside. Even when he was a child, it was a struggle for Betty to get him to do anything outside of the house. She always told him it wasn't healthy. He never listened.

"You don't look good." She shook her head as she spoke.

"Thanks, Mom. I love you too." He walked over and gave her a peck on the cheek.

"Let me heat up some food for you."

"I ate at the office."

"But Tawana makes the best chili in the city." According to everyone in the family, that was true. There was a time when Ethan wouldn't have missed eating Tawana's chili.

He hung his head wearily. "I'm tired. I'm going to head to bed. I just wanted to say hi before I went to sleep."

"It's only nine thirty."

He sighed. "It doesn't matter what time it is. I'm tired, so I'm going to sleep."

"You don't have to get snippy with me. I'm just trying to make sure you're all right." Betty pressed her lips together. She could have said more, but she already felt like she was saying too much.

"I'm not ten anymore, Mom." He walked out of the kitchen. "I'm going to bed."

Betty clutched the dish towel as she watched him walk through the living room where Tawana sat watching television and up the hall to the bedroom. She looked at Tawana, who gave her a knowing look and shook her head.

"I guess he had a bad day at work," Betty said.

"He's been having a lot of those recently." Tawana picked up the remote. "I'm going to bed too. Do you want to watch TV?"

Betty shook her head. "I'll watch the news in my bedroom."

Tawana switched off the television before standing. She stretched her arms above her head and yawned. "Good night."

Betty stood in the empty living room for a few moments. On the wall over the television hung a series of black-and-white photos of the family: Maia and Imani smiling big into the camera, their hair in matching twisted pigtails; Tawana and Ethan gazing lovingly into each other's eyes on the beach; the whole family posing for a photo in a park downtown. Betty liked that photo the best. She had a smaller version of it on her nightstand. It was only taken two years ago, but they seemed like a completely different family. The girls were so much bigger. Two years made a big difference to children.

Betty wandered through the house, turning off the lights. She always liked the nighttime when the house was quiet. Even in her own house when Ethan was young, she would stay up later than everyone else and sit outside on the back patio reading a book. She didn't read as much as she used to. There were so many channels now, you could never run out of things to watch on TV. Betty liked Hallmark movies. Those were her favorites, even though most of the time she knew what was going to happen. There was comfort in that.

In her bedroom, she shuffled around, turning on the television and putting on her nightgown. She kept the volume low, even though it was hard for her to hear, because she didn't want to wake anyone else in the house. She was piling up the pillows against her headboard so she could sit up and watch television comfortably when she heard a beep coming from her purse. Years ago, Ethan had bought her a small flip phone. He wanted her to carry it in case of emergencies. She could count on one hand the number of times she'd used it. The buttons were so tiny she could barely see them. When she had used it, she doubted if it would really work. Most of the time it lay in her purse untouched, except for when it beeped, telling her it needed charging.

It had taken her a while to learn to do that, but once she had run into trouble downtown and the battery was dead. That was when she was still driving. She got into her car only to find it wouldn't start. She had no way to call anyone to help her because the phone had no charge. Luckily, she met a nice woman in the parking lot who gave her car a jump, but when she told Tawana about it, she was angry. "That's why we gave you the phone," Tawana had said. She taught Betty how to charge the phone, sticking the cord into a tiny little spot in the bottom. It was so hard to see, but she knew she had to make sure she kept it charged just in case.

Betty scooted off the bed and padded over to her purse sitting on the chair in the far corner of the room. She dug through the bag, looking for the phone amongst the lipstick, wads of Kleenex, and a lot of loose change. When she found it, she took the smooth plastic phone out, and just as she was going to close the purse, she noticed something else--a folded piece of paper. It looked like it had been in there for years. She pulled the crinkled white paper out and carefully unfolded it. On the front was written a phone number--Sam's phone number when he still lived with his dad. She recognized the large, loopy handwriting as belonging to her younger self.

"How strange," Betty said to herself. She sat in the chair, her hand shaking. "How did this get into my purse?" A chill traveled the length of her spine as she remembered the dream she had that afternoon. "It can't be." A lump rose in her throat. It couldn't be possible.

Chapter Four

THE shrill ring of the telephone cut through the air. Sam answered it, expecting to hear his father on the other end. "Hello?"

"May I speak to Sam, please?"

He recognized the voice immediately. "Betty?"

"Sam?"

"You're speaking to the one and only." He grinned as he spoke.

She chuckled. "Sam is a common name. I'm sure there are thousands, maybe even millions."

"You're speaking to one of millions, then."

She laughed again.

"How are you doing?" He wasn't just making small talk. He wanted to know. He wanted to know everything he possibly could about her.

"Good." She paused for a moment. "I'm calling to tell you about Tucker's going-away party. I'd love to see you there, if you still want to go."

Sam hated that name now. He wished she would never say it to him. He wanted to pretend that Tucker didn't exist at all. "Oh, yeah, the party. Where is it?"

Betty told him the address, what to expect, and what to wear. He listened attentively. Once she was done telling him about the party, he assumed the conversation would end, but something amazing happened. She kept talking.

She wanted to know about him, what he wanted to do in the future and what he cared about.

"What do you think you'll be doing in ten years?" she asked.

"I don't know."

"What do you mean, you don't know? You don't ever think about it? I think about it all the time." There was an urgency in her voice.

"What do you think you'll be doing in ten years, then?" He wanted to know about her more than he wanted to talk about himself.

"Everybody thinks I'll get married to Tucker when he comes back from Korea and we'll have kids, but I'm not so sure about that."

"You're not? What do you want to do, then?"

She was quiet for a moment.

"Is it a secret?" he teased.

"No. I want to work. I'm going to secretarial school." She paused, and Sam wondered if she was waiting for him to say something.

"That's good. I think you'd make a good secretary."

"You don't think it's improper for a woman to work?"

Sam never really thought about it at all before that moment. "No. Most of my teachers were women. They were working."

"That's right." He could hear the smile in her voice. "That's what I'll tell Tucker the next time he tells me women shouldn't work." She paused. "It's scary that Tucker is going off to war, but if I'm honest about it, part of me is relieved.

I need a break, but I don't want to hurt his feelings."

"You should tell him if you don't want to go steady anymore. Doing that is better than stringing him along." Even though he wanted desperately for them to break up, Sam felt badly for Tucker.

"I probably should, but it seems like a cruel thing to do just before he leaves for war. We're friends, even if I'm not sure I love him."

Sam swallowed hard. "If you are friends, you should tell him the truth before he goes."

"It's too mean. I can't. He's already talking about how much he'll look forward to my letters when he's gone." She cleared her throat. "Do you think you'll get married and have kids?"

"I guess. That's what normal people do."

"So, you think of yourself as normal?" She giggled.

"What's that supposed to mean?"

"Nothing."

"Tell me." He listened expectantly, hoping what she said would be good.

"You aren't normal, Sam. You're extraordinary." Laughter peppered her speech, leaving him wondering if she was making fun of him.

"So are you."

She went quiet again, this time for so long that he started to think the line had disconnected.

"Hello?"

"I'm still here," she said.

His chest tightened. "I knew you were extraordinary as soon as I saw you at the ice cream parlor." He waited for her to say something, and when she didn't, he kept on talking. "You shouldn't stay with Tucker if you don't want to. You're too good for him."

"You don't know that. Tucker is a nice guy."

Sam doubted that. Tucker always seemed smug and full of himself to him. "I think you'd make a good secretary, and if that's what you want to do, you should. You can do anything you want to do."

"You wouldn't say that if you saw me trying to master the triple dismount two years ago."

"The triple what?"

"Dismount. It's where you twist in the air and then you land on your feet from the uneven bars. I could never nail it. I was always falling over."

Sam was confused. "Wait a minute, what are you talking about?"

"Gymnastics. I was a gymnast for years, ever since I was eight years old. I had to quit last year because I just couldn't do it anymore. I wasn't getting any better. It was frustrating, and my coach kept telling me I was just too tall. When I was younger, all I wanted to do was get taller, and then it ruined my gymnastics career."

"You're not that tall."

"Tall enough to make a difference. It's fine. I don't even worry about it because I was kind of over gymnastics anyway. It was taking up too much of my time, and there are other things I want to do."

"Like what?"

"You ask a lot of questions, Sam." Happiness bounced through her voice.

"I only ask questions I want to know the answers to."

"At the time, I wanted to learn how to ride horses. Unfortunately, it didn't happen. My parents said riding lessons were too expensive. Then I started dating Tucker, and that took up a lot of time. You know how it is when you're dating someone."

"Yeah, relationships take a lot of time." Sam had a steady girlfriend once. Her name was Julia, and she spoke with a lisp that he thought was cute.

"You never told me what you wanted to do."

"My dad thinks I'll take over the sandwich shop, but I don't really want to do that. I want to help people. I'm not quite sure how yet. I was going to college in Tampa until I was drafted. I was thinking that while I was in Korea, I'd probably be able to figure out something more concrete that I wanted to do." He scowled at himself in the mirror. "I want to help poor people around the world. Maybe that sounds naïve--"

She broke in before he could even finish what he was saying. "That doesn't sound naïve at all. It sounds wonderful. I think it's great that you want to help people. Most people just think about what they can get for themselves."

"I'm not most people."

"That you're not."

Sam and Betty talked for more than an hour, and after they finally hung up, he thought about her the rest of the day.

He was still thinking about that phone call while he stood outside of the diner Tucker's parents had rented for the party. Sam listened to the ruckus inside as he stood looking through the large plate glass window in the front of the restaurant. There didn't seem to be any parents there. Kids danced together in the open space where the tables once were and sat at the booths eating hamburgers and fries. Arthur, the owner of the diner, stood behind the counter dancing, waving a spatula in the air and singing along with the music.

Betty twirled on the dance floor as Tucker spun her, her full skirt flicking up and revealing her shapely legs. Her light brown hair shone under the lights. Tucker flipped her in the air like she weighed nothing, and everyone clapped and cheered.

Sam wished he could dance like that with her. His mother had tried to teach him when he was little, but he had two left feet and no sense of rhythm. Watching him dance was like watching a fish run a marathon.

Before he pushed open the door of the diner, he replayed the phone call in his head to build his confidence. Even though Betty was with Tucker, he could tell she liked him.

There was a group of kids crowding the doorway, bobbing their heads to the beat of the music. Sam excused himself and maneuvered through them. Immediately he saw someone he knew, Kevin Beecher. His white-blond hair was combed up into a pompadour that looked ridiculous on him.

"Samuel!" Kevin came over and gave him a hug and a handshake. "I heard you were drafted too. My number hasn't come up yet, but I think it'll probably be soon."

"Probably." Sam searched the crowd for Betty. She'd stopped dancing, and he had lost sight of her for a moment.

Noticing, Kevin looked over his shoulder. "Are you looking for someone?"

Sam shook his head quickly. "There're a lot of people here."

"Tucker's popular."

"Yeah, he always has been. I guess that happens when you play varsity basketball."

Kevin smiled widely. "Or when your parents are wealthy."

"That too," Sam said. He finally spotted Betty at the far side of the diner in a fuzzy sweater and a bright red skirt. Tucker's arm draped over her shoulder as they talked to three girls who all seemed to be flirting with Tucker even though Betty was standing right there. "I want to go talk to the guest of honor."

Kevin turned around and saw Tucker standing with all the girls. "He's busy."

"I have to be polite." Sam made a beeline through the crowd. Betty saw him coming across the room. Sam looked directly into her eyes as he approached; his smile was determined.

"I wonder if they play basketball in Korea," Tucker was saying when Sam got to the edge of the group he was talking to.

"They must. They play basketball everywhere," a short girl in a tight white sweater and capri pants said.

"Any place where they don't play basketball is a place I don't want to go to." Tucker laughed and looked over at Betty, who was smiling shyly at Sam. Noticing Betty's gaze wasn't focused on him, Tucker followed her line of sight until his eyes landed squarely on Sam. "Don't I know you?"

"You must. Otherwise, he wouldn't be at your party," the girl in the white sweater said.

"I've seen you around," Sam said, not missing a beat. "But don't think we've ever talked."

"What are you doing here, then?" He wasn't being defensive. Instead, he seemed confused.

Betty put her hand around his waist. "I invited Sam. He's shipping out the same day you are."

"No kidding. Isn't it something else how they're making us all go over there? What does what's happening on the other side of the world have to do with me? I was getting ready to go to school on a basketball scholarship."

"It's our duty to help others get the freedom we have. Do you want the commies taking over the world?" Other people in the group nodded in agreement with Sam.

"Of course I don't. I'm going to serve. It's my duty. I'm happy to do it. I was just asking a question."

A fast song came on and the music washed over them like a tidal wave.

"You're such a good dancer, Tucker," the girl in the white sweater said. She looked over at Betty. "I hope you don't mind if I ask him to dance with me just this one last time before he leaves."

Betty faked a pout, poking out her lip, before breaking into a smile. "Go ahead."

The girl grabbed Tucker's hand and pulled him out onto the dance floor. He twirled her around at the end of this arm and pulled her in like a yo-yo. As soon as Tucker got on the dance floor, everyone's attention turned to him, including Sam's. He watched as they danced, wishing he could do that too.

A light touch on his shoulder took his attention away from the dancing.

"Come outside with me," Betty said. "I need to get away from this noise."

Sam had to strain to hear what she said. The music seemed to have gotten louder once Tucker started dancing.

Sam followed Betty out the back door and into the alley. A pink haze hung in the early evening sky, and a river of dirty water ran down the center of the alley. They sat on overturned wooden crates.

Betty let out a groan. "I swear I've been standing since this party started."

"I don't know why. There were plenty of seats in there."

"Yeah, but most of them are taken."

"The whole time?" He smirked.

"Of course not, smarty-pants. That's not going to make girls like you."

"Should I be trying to make you like me? I mean, you have a boyfriend."

Betty shrugged. "Right now."

"Right now? So, you're going to tell him?"

"Probably not. It will break his heart."

"From what I've seen, he has no shortage of girls interested in him."

"Are you saying I'm easily replaceable?" She lightly punched his arm.

"No one could replace you."

"I couldn't. People would think I was terrible for breaking up with him now," she said.

"Do you care what people think?"

"No." There was a twinkle of mischief in her eye.

"That's what I thought."

"I'm too young to know what I want."

"I know exactly what I want, Betty."

Betty flushed and looked down at her lap for a moment. When she looked up again, her gaze met his.

"I'm going to win you over," he declared.

"You'll have to work hard to do that."

The door clicked open and a gaggle of laughing people spilled out, followed by a cascade of music. Sam felt like he'd been caught doing something wrong. He jumped up off his crate and shoved his hands in his pockets. "I should go."

Betty stood. The crowd started up the alley, talking and laughing loudly.

"Maybe you should."

He looked at her again, trying to read her face. Had he offended her?

Tucker popped his head out the door. "There you are. I was looking all over for you."

"Tucker," Betty stammered. "Sam was just leaving."

Tucker glanced over at Sam and raised his head in a kind of reverse nod. "You just got here."

"I just stopped in for a minute." Sam didn't like him. He didn't like him at all. "I have to go help my dad with his business."

"Okay then. It was good meeting you. I'll probably see you again." Tucker reached out his hand and took Betty's small hand in his. "Come on inside."

The moment they'd had alone and the feeling that was tucked inside of it vanished. Sam watched as Tucker pulled Betty back inside. He walked down the alley alone, his hands shoved in his pockets.

Chapter Five

BETTY woke up in the morning with sticky fingers and sore feet. Her muscles ached like she hadn't slept at all. In the blurry moments between sleeping and waking, she thought she saw Sam sitting in the flowered chair in front of her window.

"Good morning, Sam," she said dreamily. When the reality of what she was seeing hit her, she opened her eyes wide and sat up. Fully alert, she realized no one was there. The chair was empty, as it should have been.

She must have thought she saw Sam in her room because of the dreams she'd been having and what Maia had said the other day. The phone number in her purse and the way her feet ached after dreaming of dancing all night were all coincidences. The mind could be so suggestible.

After she showered and dressed, she went into the kitchen, following the girls' light laughter and her son's voice rumbling through the air.

"Good morning," Tawana said. She stood at the counter spooning scrambled eggs onto several white plates. When each plate was filled with food, Imani took it to the table.

Ethan sat at the far end of the table in front of the

window, looking down at his cell phone. A plate piled high with scrambled eggs and home-fried potatoes sat in front of him. When Betty entered the room, he looked up and smiled. He looked so much like his father when he smiled that sometimes it made Betty want to weep. He was tall with the lanky frame of a runner, even though he never ran. His sport of choice had always been tennis, and he hardly ever played anymore. Still wet from the shower, his dark brown hair was combed back off his forehead. The lines left by the comb's teeth were still visible. A piece of tissue dotted with blood stuck to his chin.

"Good morning, Mom. I'm glad you're up in time to join us for breakfast. I was afraid you'd sleep in, and I'd miss you."

"You've made my morning." Betty was worried that he might be angry with her after their conversation the night before, but Ethan was always a lot better at forgiving and forgetting than she was. He'd gotten that quality from his father.

"That was easy." He snorted.

"It's been so long since you've joined us for breakfast." She hurried over to the table and kissed him on his forehead, just like she used to when he was a boy.

Tawana carried another plate over and set it on the table. "I assume you're joining us."

"Of course." Betty sat in the chair across from Ethan. The girls were already eating.

"Does this mean the project you're working on is finished?" Betty asked Ethan.

Ethan had already returned his attention to his phone. He cleared his throat and looked up again. "Yeah, we finished it up last night."

"That's good. Congratulations. So, you'll be around the house more, then?"

Ethan pursed his lips. "I don't know. Jenkins has another project he wants me on."

Betty didn't even know what Ethan did, but she knew Jenkins was his boss. "I guess that's good, because it means you did well on the last one, right?"

"That's right. If I keep this up, I'll move up again in no time. That would mean a significant pay raise." He looked back at Tawana. "It'll also mean more time at the office, but I think it will be worth it."

Betty wondered if it really would be worth it. "I'm glad you like your job, but you have to consider your family too."

"That's why I'm doing this, for Tawana and the girls." He pressed his lips into a tight line. "For you too."

Betty glanced at Tawana, who ate her eggs in silence. She tried to make eye contact with her, but Tawana was watching the girls.

"The girls really need to have a father around. You're missing all the best parts of their lives. If you're gone any more, Tawana might as well be a single mother."

Ethan cocked his head at Betty. She could see the steam building behind his eyes and knew he might blow. She shouldn't have said what she'd said, but she couldn't help herself.

"Mother, we enjoy having you stay with us, and I realize that living here might make you feel like that gives you the right to tell us how to raise our family, but this is my family, and you're here as a guest."

"Is Daddy mad?" Maia asked. "Are you fighting?"

"Shhh." Imani held her finger to her mouth and shushed Maia.

"Granddad says you shouldn't talk to Grandma like that. He didn't raise you that way," Maia said.

Ethan looked at her small face, his lips slightly parted.

"What did you say?"

"She thinks she sees Granddad now, but she can't because he's dead." Imani took a bite of her eggs. "Mom told her to stop, but she won't."

Ethan looked at Tawana, his forehead creased. "How long has this been going on?"

"Since yesterday," Tawana told her husband before turning her attention to her youngest daughter. "Maia, I told you this isn't funny."

Maia's eyes widened, and she nodded. "Granddad said he doesn't mean for it to be funny. He wants to make sure Ethan--" She looked around at all of them at the table before her gaze settled on her father. "--Dad doesn't throw his family away." She bit her lip. "You're going to throw us away?"

"No, of course not." Ethan shifted in his chair. "I love you, all of you." He made eye contact with each of the girls. "I'm not going anywhere."

"You're going to work in a few minutes." Imani's fork scraped as she pushed bits of egg around on her plate.

"That's not what I mean." Ethan looked at Tawana as if asking for help.

"Granddad says you'd better wise up." Maia emphasized "up" by raising her fork over her head.

Betty and Ethan looked at each other for a moment before Ethan said, "That's exactly what Dad would say."

Betty nodded, and she swore she felt a feathery touch on her neck. She raised her hand, putting her palm over the sensitive part of the skin on the back of her neck where the feeling lingered. She looked at each member of her family sitting at the table. "Did you feel that?"

Bewildered eyes met her question.

"What?" Tawana asked.

Betty shook her head. "Nothing."

"Granddad says——" Maia began.

"We're through talking about this now." Tawana's voice was stern.

"I want to hear what he said." Ethan's voice was light, but his eyes betrayed his concern.

"Forget it. He told me not to tell you." Maia bobbed her head, as if keeping time to a song only she could hear as she went back to eating.

"That's not fair." Ethan's boyishness peeked through, and Betty remembered how lively he was as a child. "I want to know what he said. You can't start a sentence and then not finish it."

"I can't tell you." An impish grin slid across Maia's face. "I can't tell you ever in a million years."

"That's a long time," Imani said. "You'll be the oldest people in the world before she can tell you."

"I guess we'll have to wait a million, then." Ethan reached over and tickled Maia's belly.

She spasmed with laughter, her arms and legs flailing as she fell on the floor.

"If you keep that up, she might choke to death," Imani said.

Tawana laughed. "You are too much, Imani."

Ethan tickled Imani too, and both girls rolled around on the floor laughing.

The rest of the breakfast was pleasant. Ethan directed the conversation at the girls, who happily informed him about their friends. Imani was making a volcano for science class and was thrilled to tell him about the chemical reaction baking soda and vinegar had, which she would use to make the lava. Maia wasn't interested in talking about homeschooling, but she'd started doing more drawing recently and had a pile of them to show him. She ran to her room and came out with stacks of paper blooming with color. She showed them to her father, not noticing as she smudged them with her greasy fingers.

"Don't you miss times like this when you're working all that overtime?" Betty knew she shouldn't bring it up again, but she saw Ethan so little these days that she couldn't hold her tongue.

Everyone looked at her. The creased look on Ethan and Tawana's faces let her know that they'd prefer she didn't talk about it, but she continued.

"There are so many things I would've done differently if I realized your father would die when he did."

Betty vividly remembered the day he told her about the cancer. Ethan and Tawana were visiting for the holidays. That was when they were still living in Denver, so they hardly saw them at all. Imani was just a baby then. They were all cleaning up after dinner when Sam announced that he had to talk to all of them. She could tell by his serious, flat tone that it was something important, but she never imagined what.

Betty sat on the sofa cradling Imani when he told them he had stage four melanoma. She didn't realize how serious it was until later. He hadn't been sick. He'd seemed just fine until he told them about the cancer. Then he faded away all at once. Three weeks after he told them about it, he was gone. It was almost as if talking about it made him sick. He went from running every morning to lying in a hospital bed, and then he was gone. It was all so fast. Betty tried to tell herself that there were plenty of people who had it worse. They'd lost loved ones in an accident or a mass shooting. At least she had a few weeks to say goodbye.

"You can't get the time back once it's gone. There are so many things I regret. I wish your father, and I had spent more time together."

Ethan's expression was growing increasingly sour. "You should've left that other guy, what was his name?"

"Tucker," Betty said, remembering her dreams.

"You should've left Tucker earlier and married Dad," Ethan said. He'd heard the story about how Betty was with someone else when she and Sam met from his father many times. Sam liked to tell the story about how he'd won her over after the war. He always said he'd stolen her from some other guy. That was kind of the way it happened. Betty was only staying with that other guy because she felt obligated after he came home from Korea injured. Stealing her away wasn't hard because she wanted to be stolen. Sam knew that from the start.

"I should've." It was like a light went on in Betty's head.

"But you can't, so this discussion is useless," Ethan said.

"Not for you though. I'm saying all of this for your benefit. The girls are only this age once."

"Well thanks, Mom. I can manage my own life though."

"I know you can. I'm just giving some motherly advice. I have been on the planet longer than you, and I've learned a few lessons."

*

After breakfast, Ethan went off to work, and Tawana took Imani to school while Betty stayed at home with Maia. Tawana had told Betty to help Maia with her math. It was simple addition, but Betty wasn't in the mood to drill her on it. Instead, she let Maia pull out her paints. They covered the kitchen table with butcher paper, and Maia painted while Betty loaded the dishwasher.

Maia sang a little song as she painted. The words rose over the rush of the running water and clinking dishes.

"What's that you're singing?" Betty asked.

Maia shrugged like she didn't know before finally answering. "I don't know the name, but I learned it in school before I stopped going. It's about friends." She started singing again. "Make new friends but keep the old."

"That's a nice song." Betty remembered learning it when she was a child. "Is it your favorite?"

She finished singing it before she answered. "No. I just sing it because one day I'm going to make friends."

Her words caught Betty off guard. She and Tawana often talked about how worrying it was that Maia didn't seem to get along with other children. She was too loud and hyper, didn't understand how to take turns, and sharing was difficult, leaving her friendless. Maia was never invited to the birthday parties of the other children in her classes when she was in school.

The homeschool kids were different in ways. Some had similar social problems as Maia, but she found no one she clicked with in the group. More often than not, she sat and played by herself, only talking to Tawana. She didn't even acknowledge the other parents. It made Tawana so sad, but there wasn't much she could do about it. Betty had told her as much when she caught her sitting in the driveway in the car crying long after bringing the girls home one day after school. She'd witnessed some other girls bullying Maia on the playground, and it had broken her heart.

"You will make friends one day. You have to give it time."

Maia looked at her with such focus that it made Betty feel a bit uncomfortable. "I will," she said, determination glinting in her eyes.

"You will." Betty wanted more than anything to make all of this better. If she could snap her fingers and give Maia's friends, she would. It was impossible to take the pain away from the ones she loved. She could only guide them and be there for them when they fell.

When she was pregnant with Ethan, she had no idea how much heartbreak would come with loving someone that much. As their family increased, that love grew, and so did the heartaches. If she had a choice, if she could just take all this pain away, she knew she would.

Maia kicked her legs as she painted on a new blank sheet of paper: five circles, some blue and some yellow, connected by a thin red line.

Chapter Six

THERE were so many clocks that Betty didn't know how Pat could even sleep in the room with all the ticking. They hung in rows on the walls, arms outstretched like cheerleaders and pendulums swinging to and fro. Their faces, absent of emotion, reminded her of time slipping away. No matter how many times Betty had been in Pat's apartment, she never tired of looking at them. She'd stand and examine the wooden clocks with intricate leaves and pinecones carved into their bodies, metal ones whose brass parts shone like the gleaming noonday sun, and modern clocks with glass panels that exposed their innards.

Each time, she discovered a new one. "This is interesting. Where did Bernie get this one?" Betty pointed to a blue-and-white clock made of thin porcelain sitting on the shelf. The numbers were painted on its face in bold black font.

Pat walked over and looked at it for a few moments before answering. "I want to say it's Eastern European, Croatian maybe. Honestly, I don't know. Bernie traveled so much for work, and he always came home with a different clock. Keeping track was hard. This isn't even half of what he had. We sold most of them when we got this place. You should've seen our house in Pennsylvania. It was stuffed to the brim with clocks."

Betty imagined grandfather clocks standing all in a row at attention, wall-mounted clocks hanging on every surface, and freestanding clocks cluttering up mantles and bookshelves. She pictured pieces of clocks littering the floors and stepping over cogs and springs to walk from the living room to the kitchen. She couldn't even begin to imagine all the noise. Being in Pat's tiny apartment on the hour was nearly deafening. She was surprised the neighbors hadn't complained, but most people in the building had nearly lost their hearing anyway. That's why the TVs blared as you walked down the hall. From each room, competing news programs and game shows bombarded passersby.

"I'm surprised you kept as many as you did," she said.

"Bernie insisted." Pat looked around at the clocks on the walls. "Even though I know he's probably not coming back, I can't bear to get rid of them."

"I don't blame you. I wouldn't be able to do it either." Betty thought about how long she kept Sam's clothes after he died. His closet was full of pants and shirts and suits that reminded her of pieces of their lives. It felt wrong to put them out. Sometimes when she missed him, she would step into the closet and soak in his scent. Even after the clothes stopped smelling of him, she kept them. It hurt her heart when she got rid of them to move into the apartment. Tawana helped her go through the clothes, and Betty kept a few of his favorite shirts to keep him close to her.

"Are you ready to go?" Pat walked to the door before Betty answered. "Bernie would love to see you. He doesn't get many visitors, just me. The change might be nice."

This was Betty's first-time seeing Bernie since he'd been in the nursing home. The idea of seeing him fading away brought a sadness to her that she didn't want to face.

Pat drove them, slowly. Traffic zoomed by. Angry drivers beeped their horns.

The nursing home had an antiseptic absence of character. The scuffed tile floors were light gray with flecks of something that sparkled. The plain white walls of the hallway featured dark scuff marks at about waist height. The staff rushed about like they were late for something in mint-green and white uniforms that reminded Betty of the cotton candy she used to get at the carnival when she was a child. The building smelled like sickness--pungent and attacking the senses from every direction. Betty swore she could feel the death on her skin. This was another reason why she had never visited Bernie. It was a place where people were sent to wait to die. Even though Betty knew death would come to her eventually, the idea of living out her last days in a place like this made her queasy.

Noise flooded the hallway through open doors, combining in a muddied puddle of sound. Betty peered into rooms as they passed and saw people with withered bodies lying in hospital beds. Pat walked so quickly; Betty could hardly keep up.

When they got to Bernie's room, the door was open just a crack. Pat gave it a light tap before pushing it open and walking inside. There were three clocks on the shelf next to his bed--a cuckoo, a simple square clock with clean lines, and a brass one protected by a glass dome.

Bernie sat propped up in bed. His eyes were closed and his head bowed forward, his chin nearly touching his chest. His lips parted slightly, releasing the heavy breath of sleep. His silver hair stuck up in all directions like it had not been combed. Thick stubble rose up from his cheeks, chin, and neck. He wore a pair of light blue pajamas. The thin mint-green hospital blanket was pulled up to his chest. A single foot stuck out of the bottom of the blanket covered in a thick gray sock. His open hands rested on his belly.

"He's sleeping," Betty said, stating the obvious. "Should we disturb him?"

Pat rested her hand on his shoulder. "Bernie, you have company."

He stirred, snorting, grunting, and smacking his lips before finally opening his eyes. His thick eyelashes fluttered before his eyelids popped open. At first, fear flashed across his face.

"Bernie, it's me, Pat, your wife. This is Betty. You remember her, don't you?" Pat put her face close to his as she spoke, as if trying to get him to focus on her.

He shook his head slowly at first, but it steadily became faster, more violent.

"Bernie, I'm right here. Look at me. I'm your wife. Do you remember me?" Her voice was firm, as if correcting a child.

Standing watching this, Betty's heart sank. She wanted to turn around and walk out the door. She wasn't ready to see her friend in this state.

"Bernie." Pat squeezed his shoulder, and that snapped him out of it.

He stilled. "Patricia?" he said, his voice hoarse, his eyes searching the room for a focal point like he couldn't see her just inches from him.

"That's right." Pat nodded, a smile spreading across her face. She stood up straight and stepped back, motioning at Betty like a game show host. "Look who came to see you."

Betty stepped forward, putting on her best smile. "Hi, Bernie. It's been a long time."

Bernie blinked a few times, and Betty thought he didn't recognize her. "Betty Boop boop be doop," he sang, pointing his index fingers from one side to the other with each word.

Betty let out a relieved laugh, and the tension melted from the room. Pat sat down in the chair next to the bed and motioned for Betty to sit in the chair on the other side.

"I thought my lovely wife was the only one who cared enough to visit me. Now I'm in the company of two beautiful women. It's almost too much for me to handle."

"Nonsense. I know about your playboy past," Betty teased.

Pat let out a belly laugh. "Everybody knows about your past, Bernie."

"I'm trying to pass out compliments, and you two are bringing up the past." He shook his head and rolled his eyes playfully.

"How have you been today?" Pat asked.

"So far, so good." He looked at Pat with his gray eyes, and she reached over and put her hand on his.

"I'm glad. Yesterday was pretty bad."

"Did you come around yesterday?"

"I come around every day." Pat's voice quivered.

"You're such a good wife."

"I love you, that's why."

They sat there gazing at each other for a few moments. Betty turned her attention to the view out the window, which was of a dark green city dumpster and the brick wall of the neighboring building.

"I don't have any news. Nothing happens around here. Why don't you tell us about what's happening with you, Betty?" Bernie said.

"Well," Betty said, not sure what to say. "We still play cards at the Starlight Café, but you already know that."

"Where is that?" A cloud of confusion passed over his face.

"You know the Starlight Café." Pat gave Betty a nervous glance. "It's your favorite coffee shop."

He waggled his lower jaw back and forth for a moment, thinking. "Oh yes. I remember now."

"My granddaughters are growing like weeds. Do you remember them?"

Bernie wrinkled his face and looked skyward. "Not really."

"I have two. They're nine and seven. The nine-year-old is so serious, and the baby is a spitfire. My daughter-in-law is homeschooling her because she was having too much trouble in school."

"A lot of people do that these days. Our daughter is homeschooling her boys," Pat said. "I don't know why she's doing it. It's not like the schools in her area are bad. I figure that, as long you're paying taxes, you might as well send your kids to public school. I mean, that's what you're paying for, right?"

"I see what you're saying, but if your kid has special needs, homeschooling can be a good option. It's working out for Maia. Tawana struggles with it a bit, but Maia is doing well." When Tawana and Ethan first said they would start homeschooling Maia, Betty thought it was a bad idea. She didn't understand the purpose of doing such a thing, but now that she had seen Maia's progress, she changed her mind.

"What else?" Bernie asked.

"I don't know." Betty paused. "I've been having the strangest dreams."

"What kind of dreams?" Pat asked.

"About Sam and when we first met."

"I dream about my past all the time." Bernie moved his legs back and forth in the bed.

"These dreams are different though. When I wake up, it's like they happened." Betty reached into her purse and pulled out the piece of paper she had found. "Look at this." She handed it to Pat, who unfolded it and took a look at the number scrawled across the front.

"What's this?"

"It's Sam's phone number from when we were young, and he still lived with his dad. I found it in my purse the other day." Betty had been puzzling over the piece of paper since she found it.

"Well, it's in your handwriting, so I don't see what the big mystery is. You must've written it down, put it in your purse, and forgot it." Pat shook her head as she spoke.

Betty wondered what that meant. "Yeah, it's my handwriting, but better. It's the way I used to write when I was young. These days my handwriting is a little bit shaky."

"Maybe you wrote it on a good day," Bernie added.

"I don't know how good the day was if I don't remember writing it." Betty reached out her hand to Pat, who handed the paper back to her. "Yesterday, I dreamed about that party we had for Tucker before he went to Korea. Remember that?"

"I sure do," Pat said. "I danced all night."

"So did I, apparently, because when I woke up this morning, my feet were sore, and my legs hurt like I'd been dancing too."

"What do you mean?" Pat cocked her head at her.

Betty had no idea what she was trying to say. It had been so strange, and she hadn't had a chance to talk about it with anyone.

"I think she's saying she's traveling back in time in her dreams." Bernie let out a laugh that sounded more like a cough.

It was kind of funny, but that was precisely what she was trying to say. That was what she was thinking in the back of her mind, even if she didn't want to say as much.

"I know because it's happened to me too," Bernie announced.

Pat and Betty looked at him with shocked eyes. "What are you talking about? You never told me anything like this." Pat's forehead wrinkled.

"I already know I'm losing it. I don't want to tell you things that'll make you think I'm losing it even faster than you already do." Bernie held out his hand, and Pat grabbed hold of it. "I don't want you to worry any more than you have to."

"Thanks, but whenever this kind of thing happens to you, you need to tell me. You need to tell the doctor." Pat was clearly concerned.

"From now on, I will. I don't think this has anything to do with me being sick though."

"I hope it doesn't, because I don't want to--" Betty stopped talking, realizing what she was about to say would've been insensitive.

They both looked at her, waiting for her to finish her sentence.

"I don't think it has anything to do with that." Betty thought it was best to keep her thoughts about illness to herself.

"Of course not. The more likely scenario is that you're time-traveling in your dreams." Pat's voice dripped was sarcasm.

"Forget it." Betty knew she shouldn't have mentioned it.

"Don't forget it," Bernie said. "You made me feel much better knowing you're having these experiences too."

"What do you dream about?" Betty wanted to take some of the attention away from herself.

"Most recently, I dreamed of getting lost in the woods when I was nine. It felt so real that when I woke up, I was in a panic."

"It was just a nightmare. We all have those." Pat's voice was so sure.

"When I woke up, I noticed something was sticking me in the ankle. I looked under the blanket, and there were burrs stuck to the hem of my pajama pants. Where would those have come from?" Bernie was just as sure what he dreamed was real as Pat seemed to be that it was not.

"I don't know, but there must be a reasonable explanation." Pat's stare was hard-edged and stern.

"We've given you the explanation." Bernie's voice was just as stern.

"Time travel is not an explanation."

Betty didn't want to see them fight. "Either way, it doesn't really matter now." Before either of them could say anything else, Betty started talking about a recent story she saw on the news about a dog that saved his family from a burning building. It was the least controversial subject she could think of. There was no way they could argue about that.

They visited Bernie for about an hour and a half, and he was in a good mood the whole time. Betty had been so afraid of visiting him, but she saw her fears were unfounded.

"He's doing better than I thought he would be," Betty said as she and Pat walked into the afternoon sun.

"This is just a good day. I live for the good days." Pat unlocked the car doors, and they got in. "I didn't appreciate all your talk about time travel. It's not good to encourage him."

"I'm sorry. I didn't mean to. It's just that I've been going through this, and I haven't had anyone to talk to about it."

"You really think you're traveling back in time in your dreams? That's not something you should be telling people." Pat started the car without looking over at Betty.

"You're probably right."

*

Tawana sat on the sofa looking through a stack of mail. She looked up when Betty walked into the house. "I didn't expect you back this early."

Betty sank into the brown leather lounge chair next to the couch and leaned her cane against its arm. "Pat had some errands to run, but I was in a lot of pain and just thought I should get home."

"Do you want me to get your painkillers?" She set the junk mail on the coffee table. She had disappeared down the hallway before Betty could answer.

Betty closed her eyes for a moment, and it seemed like only seconds had passed before she opened them again to see Tawana standing before her with a glass of water in hand.

Tawana handed her two pain pills and the glass before returning to the sofa. Betty took the two small pills before closing her eyes. As long as she kept her mind occupied, the pain was easier to bear.

"Do you have any regrets?" she asked Tawana.

Tawana looked up from the mail. "Of course I do. Doesn't everyone?"

"I assume so. I definitely do." Betty opened her eyes and watched Tawana as she sorted the mail into keep and recycle piles on the coffee table in front of her. "If you could change those things, would you?"

"Probably not. You know what they say about the choices you made in the past making the person you are now. I'm pretty pleased with the person I am now."

"What if you could change one little thing to spend more time with someone you love?"

"You mean like telling my father not to get in the car the

day he died in that wreck?"

"That's exactly what I mean."

"I would do it." She didn't hesitate.

"Would it be the right thing to do? I mean, every choice affects the way the future is now. How would your future be different if your father was still alive? Maybe that would make it so you never married Ethan and never had the girls. Is that something you'd be willing to sacrifice?"

"There's no way of knowing if that's what it would mean. I would have loved to have had my dad around longer. I guess I'd be willing to accept whatever the consequences of that were." She looked over at the family picture hanging on the wall. She was quiet for a while, as if trying to imagine life without Ethan and her daughters. "Maybe I wouldn't. If it meant losing them, I wouldn't."

"Before I married Sam, I dated the young man who was a high school basketball star."

"Tucker, right?"

Betty nodded. "I wasted a lot of time with him because I felt obligated. When he came back from the war, he was hurt pretty badly, and I felt like I couldn't break up with him then. I came this close to marrying him." She held up her thumb and index finger only an inch apart. "I mean really close. I bought a dress, and we had the church booked."

"What happened?"

"I realized that feeling obligated wasn't a good enough reason to get married."

"When did you meet Ethan's father?"

Betty thought about her dream. "I met him a week before he left for the war. I liked him right away, but I was dating someone else."

"So, when you called off your wedding, he was waiting in the wings." Tawana smirked.

"That's pretty much what happened."

"Such drama," Tawana said. "You make me and Ethan sound so boring."

"Boring is better. All the drama was too stressful. I swear I aged five years trying to make a decision."

"What was the deciding factor?"

"I didn't really love the other guy. I never did."

She nodded knowingly. "Why were you with him, then?"

"At first it was because he was popular, and he asked me out. I thought it would be fun. It was too. He was a fun guy, but he just wasn't the kind of guy for me. Then he was drafted, and I felt I couldn't leave him then. Everyone always said we were so good together and they expected us to get married and have kids. And when he came back, he was injured, and I couldn't leave him then."

"This is all kind of shocking to me. I always think of you as so assertive. I can't imagine you being pressured into dating someone you didn't really like."

"The experience of canceling the wedding, even though everyone told me not to, was one of the things that taught me to be more assertive."

Betty remembered the day so clearly. She was at the church when she decided not to do it. She hadn't yet gotten into her dress. Her mother and Pat were there. She remembered the look on their faces as she told them she wasn't going to go through with the wedding. They were all so sure she was doing the wrong thing, that she just had cold feet. Her mother had no idea what was going on, but Pat kind of did. She knew Betty had been talking to Sam.

"Did you start dating Sam right away?"

Betty nodded. "Yes. It sounds so cruel to me now, but we did our best to be discreet. We always met out of town to make sure no one we knew saw us together. We were so in love that nothing was going to stop us from seeing each other."

A cool breeze passed over Betty. She swore she heard a voice whisper, "You were worth the wait."

"Did you hear that?" Betty swiveled her head back and forth, looking for the source of the voice.

"Hear what?" Tawana pulled a piece of paper from its envelope and started ripping it to shreds. "We need to buy a new shredder." She dropped the pieces in the small white plastic trash can on the floor next to her.

"I thought I heard a voice."

"I didn't hear anything." She stood slowly. "The girls are down the street at the Andersons' house. I have to walk down there to get them."

"What if I told you I was traveling back in time in my dreams?"

"I'd tell Ethan that we need to make a doctor's appointment for you. Maybe you need a brain scan."

Betty laughed. "Like a brain scan would tell you that I'm out of my mind."

"Probably not, but I would like to get you checked out by a doctor. Are you having any problems remembering things?" Tawana squinted at Betty like her eyesight was bad.

"No. I've been fine."

She knitted her brow. "Are you sure?"

"Of course, I am. Don't worry about me. Go get the girls before the Andersons start thinking you've abandoned them."

When Tawana left, Betty closed her eyes again. The painkillers would start working soon. She couldn't wait to sleep that night. She didn't know if she would even be able to change anything in her dreams, but she wanted to try.

Chapter Seven

"I'M glad you came. I was starting to think you weren't going to show up." Sam smiled so widely that Betty thought she could see all his teeth.

"What made you think that? I'm not that late." She looked down at the watch on her wrist. The light from the streetlamp glinted on her light brown hair.

"No. I thought maybe Tucker was mad or something, so you wouldn't show up." That's all Sam had been thinking about as he waited, listening to the water lap against the sand. Many people strolled along the waterfront on this unusually chilly night. Sam put his hands into the pockets of the gray jacket he wore over his navy-blue button-down shirt.

"Tucker? Mad?" She cocked her head at him.

"Don't say it like that. You know what I mean. He's your boyfriend, and here you are going out to see another guy on the night before he heads off to war."

"He's not my boyfriend anymore." She teased out the words.

"What do you mean? You broke up with him?" Sam's heart leaped.

She nodded emphatically. "Yes, as a matter of fact, I did."

"You broke up with him on the night before he's supposed to leave for the war?"

"It sounds like you're judging me." Her voice was sharp.

"No, I'm not. I'm just wondering why you would do something like that." Sam knew exactly what he was hoping to hear.

Her gaze flitted away for a moment before returning to his. "I met someone else."

Sam's heart beat a little bit faster. He swallowed hard.

"I didn't tell Tucker that, of course. I told him he was going off to war and I was going off to school, so I thought it would be better if we didn't go steady anymore." She looked out at the water. "He didn't take it too well."

"Did you expect him to?"

She shrugged. "I don't know what I expected. Most of the time it seemed like we didn't have much in common anymore anyway. I always told people we would get married because that's what I was supposed to do, but honestly, a life married to Tucker would get old really fast. Going steady with him was already starting to get old."

Sam wondered if this was a warning sign. If life with Tucker, one of the most popular guys in school, was getting old for her, how would she feel about dating him? He wasn't a popular athlete. He was quiet and reserved. And now that he thought about it, maybe he was even boring. "If you broke up with me, I would've taken it hard too."

She smiled. "It's a good thing I'm not breaking up with you, then, isn't it?" She looked up the sidewalk that led along the waterfront. Palm trees stretched toward the sky. A white crane stood in the sand at the water's edge. The sun was just beginning to set, and couples strolled along the sidewalk hand in hand.

"Do you want to go for a walk?" He watched her profile against the streaking colors of the sunset.

"Of course, that's why you asked me to meet you here."

They strolled up the walkway near the water. The sky glowed orange and pink. At first, they didn't say much. Sam wasn't sure what to say. He couldn't believe that she'd broken up with Tucker because of him. He was surprised when she slipped her hand into the crook of his elbow, holding on to him as they walked. The scent of her sweet floral perfume rose above the briny smell of the water.

Walking with Betty was nice. He had to slow his normal pace, but he didn't mind. Her skirt swooshed as it brushed against his pants while they walked. He was too wrapped up in the moment to speak.

"You're awfully quiet," she said. Sam could feel her eyes on him.

"I was just enjoying the moment."

"It is beautiful out here, isn't it?"

He looked at her and slowed his pace even more. "I guess, but that's not what I was talking about. I was talking about walking with you. I can't think of a better way to spend my last night."

She smiled broadly, showing off a row of perfect white teeth. "You say that like you don't think you're ever coming back."

"It's a war. That is a possibility." Sam couldn't help but let on how nervous he was. He'd never shot a gun before and had always assumed he never would.

"Don't worry. You'll come back safe and sound, and we'll get married. We'll even have a son."

Sam laughed. "I don't know how I feel about this. You have everything planned out, and I haven't even kissed you yet."

She stopped. Sam did too. "What are you waiting for?"

He didn't know whether he should be worried or happy. He'd wanted to kiss her ever since he'd first seen her but thought he probably never would. She had a boyfriend who he was certain she was going to marry. It was funny how quickly things changed. Would she change her mind so quickly about him one day? There was no way of knowing, but he knew he shouldn't worry about that now. She wanted him to kiss her, and he wanted to. That was the most important thing in the moment. Tomorrow he would head off to war, and if he did kiss her, he'd have that to look back on the whole time he was gone.

He pulled her into him and kissed her. Her lips were soft and sweet and everything he had imagined.

"This is the start of something big," she whispered in his ear.

"I sure hope so," he said.

Before that night, Sam was afraid he wouldn't survive the war, but now that he had something to come home to, he knew he would. He had to if he ever wanted to see Betty again.

Chapter Eight

WHEN Betty awoke, a haze of happiness had settled across her face. Her aches and pains even seemed to have diminished for a little while.

When she opened her eyes, she noticed her room looked different. Her bed was on the wall beneath the window and her chair was gone. The beige carpet was replaced with a dark wood floor. A maroon oriental rug lay in the middle of the room.

She got out of bed as quickly as her body would allow. Her heart racing, she hurried down the hall to the kitchen without putting on her robe.

"Someone's changed my room around while I was sleeping." Even as she heard herself say the words, she knew they were crazy.

A lanky teenage boy of about fourteen sat at the kitchen table looking down at his phone, his dirty blond hair falling over his eyes. He was gangly, all legs and arms and elbows and knees. She had never seen him before, and Betty thought it was strange that they would have company so early in the morning.

Ethan sat next to the boy. He looked to have put on about twenty pounds overnight, and his chestnut brown hair was grayer than before. He looked up when Betty entered the room, the creases in his face a bit deeper. A scruffy goatee covered his chin. "What's wrong with your room?"

Betty furrowed her brows. "I didn't know we were having company for breakfast. Where are the girls?"

"What girls?" a voice behind her asked.

Betty turned around to see a statuesque blonde standing in front of the stove cooking pancakes.

"Who are you?" She looked back at Ethan, who had closed the book he'd been reading. "Who is she? Where's Tawana?"

Ethan stood up slowly. The woman put her spatula down and also started walking toward Betty. The boy stared with his mouth agape.

Betty took one step back and another at their approach.

"Where are Imani and Maia?"

"Mother, I don't know who any of these people are you're asking about. Are you feeling okay?" Ethan's voice was gentle but precise. He spoke in slow sentences like he thought Betty couldn't understand English.

She took a wobbly step backward, grabbing the doorway to steady herself. "Don't talk to me like that. I know what I'm talking about."

"Mom." The woman was speaking now. Betty could not understand why she was calling her that.

"I'm not your mom."

"You told me to call you Mom when Ethan and I first got married. You don't remember?" The woman was sure to make firm eye contact with Betty, as if she were trying to calm a frightened animal. "I'm Melissa, your daughter-in-law." Her voice rose when she said "in-law," as if she wasn't really sure herself who she was.

"Who? What?" Betty looked at Ethan, expecting him to start laughing, but his face was grave. "This isn't funny. Where are Maia and Imani?" She looked around the kitchen that was the same one she remembered. "Tawana! Tawana!"

She marched through the kitchen, past Ethan and Melissa, and into the living room. It was different than before. The round, soft furniture that Betty had spent many evenings lounging on watching television with the family was gone. A stiff black leather sofa sat in front of a glass coffee table. "What happened to all the furniture?"

Ethan and Melissa followed her.

"Nothing happened to the furniture, Mom. It's the same as it always was." Melissa tried to put her hand on Betty's shoulder, but Betty shook her off.

"Stop calling me Mom. I don't know who you are. Why are you trying to touch me?"

"I was just...." Melissa's voice trailed off, and she took a few steps back.

"Go back into the kitchen. I'll deal with this," Ethan told Melissa.

"I'm something to deal with now?" Betty swung around so she could face her son. He looked so different. "What happened to you? What's with the beard? I don't like it."

He shook his head. "I really don't want to start my morning like this. I have a busy day ahead of me. I should be leaving, but now I have to deal with this, and you're insulting me." He stopped speaking and took a few deep breaths. "I'm sorry. I know this isn't your fault."

"That's right. This is not my fault. All I did is wake up and come into the kitchen to see some strange woman where my daughter-in-law should be and my granddaughters missing." Betty peered into the kitchen.

"Your daughter-in-law is right where she needs to be. You don't have any granddaughters. You have one grandson, and his name is Casey." He nodded with each word to give it emphasis. "I know you don't like my beard. We've had this discussion many times before, but I like it, and I'm an adult who can do whatever I want with my facial hair."

Betty furrowed her brow. "What are you saying? Of course you have daughters. Two of them. I was so happy when they were born, because you waited so long to have them that I was starting to think I would never have grandchildren."

He put his hand to his forehead and gave an exasperated sigh. "I really can't do this now, Mom."

"Let me show you. Wait right here." Betty marched through the kitchen where Melissa was putting pancakes on plates and the boy, Casey, hadn't moved from his seat at the table. She went straight down the hallway to her bedroom. Standing at the doorway, she looked around, then went over to the bedside table to retrieve the family picture that she always kept there, but when she looked at it, Tawana, Maia, and Imani had been replaced by Melissa and Casey. "No. This isn't right. This can't be right." Carrying the picture, she walked back up the hallway to the kitchen, waving it around in her hand. "You replaced my picture when you changed my room around. When did you do it?"

"Mother, no one has replaced anything. I need you to calm down."

She didn't like the way Ethan talked to her. He acted like he thought she was a mental patient. She wasn't a mental patient. She knew exactly what she was talking about. This was all wrong. Everything was all wrong.

"This isn't mine. You can take it." She thrust the picture into his chest.

"Of course it's yours." He took it from her and set it on the kitchen counter.

The boy finally looked up from his phone. "What's wrong with Grandma?"

"Don't call me that. I'm not your grandma." She waved her finger around, pointing it like it was a weapon.

Ethan latched his arm in hers and started pulling her down the hall. "Come on. You need to lie down and get some rest."

Betty didn't resist much. She couldn't really. She was no match for him, especially without her cane. Frankly, getting some rest seemed like a good idea. She could lie down for a nap and wake up to find everything had returned to normal.

She laughed. "This is a dream, isn't it? This has to be a dream."

"It's not. Unfortunately, it's not." He walked her straight over to her bed where she sat down.

The springs gave under her weight. "I'm tired. Maybe I should go back to bed for a few hours."

"That sounds like a good idea. While you're sleeping, I'll call the doctor to see if he can fit you into his schedule. Hopefully he'll be able to see you today."

Betty assumed she wouldn't have much use for the doctor, so she agreed. Ethan tucked her in like she was a child. He pushed her yellow hair from her forehead and kissed her before leaving the room. She listened to him walk down the hall. Once he was in the kitchen, Betty could hear him and Melissa talking. She only caught snippets of the conversation, but she heard enough to know they were both worried. She also heard them mention putting her in a home.

She lay awake looking at the ceiling, making out shapes on the rough white surface. Faces were always so easy to find.

Shock prevented sleep. Betty lay awake for hours. She heard Ethan leave the house first, his keys jingling, his heavy footsteps on the hardwood floor. Then Melissa and Casey left a few moments later. Casey's sneakers squeaked on the tiled kitchen floor.

When the house was silent, Betty got up. She needed to sleep and hoped she'd be able to find some sleeping pills to help her get back to reality. Her ribs and hip ached when she rose to her feet. She wondered why she dreamed about being in pain. Shouldn't she be healthier in the world her mind made up? Grabbing the cane from the doorknob, she went into the bathroom. Even though she knew she had no sleeping pills, she decided to check the medicine cabinet.

Everything was just like she remembered it before she went to sleep, one bottle of aspirin, a bottle of painkillers, multivitamins, and no sleeping pills. After coming up empty-handed, she decided to wander into Ethan and Melissa's bathroom to see what she could find there. There was nothing, and her head was hurting more. She went back into her bathroom to take a painkiller before returning to bed.

She'd only just gotten back in bed when she heard the front door open and close. The footsteps were light and fast. Before she knew it, there was a knock at her door.

"Mom," Melissa said through the solid door. "Are you awake?"

"Yes." Betty had just gotten back into bed and pulled the sheets up to her chin. "You can come in."

Melissa pushed the door open a crack. "I talked to your doctor, and she wants me to bring you over right now. I hope that's okay."

"I don't think I really need to see the doctor. I feel fine." Betty never much cared for going to the doctor, and it seemed like the older she got, the more she had to go. If it were allowed, she was sure the doctor would've preferred her to just live in the office.

"We would all feel better if you did go. You've been forgetting a lot of things recently, and after this morning...." She bit her lip and looked at the floor. "I told the doctor what happened, and she said you definitely need to come in. She just wants to check you out." She twisted the doorknob in her hand, and it made a clicking sound. "Do you remember me yet?"

Betty almost shook her head, but then she realized it would probably be in her best interest to lie. That was the only way she could possibly avoid seeing the doctor. "Yes, of course. I don't know what happened this morning. I just wasn't feeling very well."

"You're better now?" She narrowed her eyes at Betty. "What year is it?"

Betty's heart thumped. "2018," she said with confidence, even though she wasn't sure if she had awoken in the past, present, or future.

"Who is the president?"

Getting the first question right instilled Betty with confidence. "Donald Trump."

"I still think you should see the doctor. Getting checked out won't hurt anything."

Betty agreed to go because Melissa was right, a checkup wouldn't hurt anything. Besides, the activity might tire her out so she could take a nap when she got home.

*

The doctor wasn't Betty's doctor, not Dr. Lamont who she had been seeing for the past twenty years. This doctor was a woman with a moon-shaped face and a serious expression. Her dark hair was pulled up into a tight bun. Her lips were the color of blood, and her eyes darkly lined. Betty found it odd that a doctor would wear that kind of makeup, but she kept her opinion to herself.

The doctor, whose name Betty did not even know, tested her reflexes and looked in her eyes and ears. She stuck a cold stethoscope on her back and asked her to breathe in and out. She listened to her heart and felt around her neck. Then she asked Betty the year and who the president was and what city they were in. Betty got all these answers correct. The doctor didn't ask the right questions. After determining that Betty was as healthy as someone with her advanced-stage osteoporosis could be, the exam was over.

"All that for nothing." Betty looked over at Melissa, who was driving the car.

Melissa looked straight ahead, her lips pressed together in a firm line. "I'm going to look for another doctor for you. We need a second opinion."

Betty's gaze traveled over Melissa, her pale skin, her thin, sharp features, the way she gripped the steering wheel like she thought it might escape. She was so unlike Tawana. She felt all wrong, and Betty could not imagine how Ethan ended up marrying her. "There's no need for that. I'm better."

"What happened this morning was serious. The doctor didn't take it seriously enough. We need to find someone else. Someone who will take better care of you. I know you've been seeing Dr. Dennison for a long time, but I think you can find someone better."

Betty saw her determination and knew that no matter what she said, Melissa would do what she wanted.

"Okay then." She wouldn't try to argue. It wasn't worth arguing over. She didn't expect to ever come back here again, so it didn't matter who her doctor was.

"I need some coffee," Melissa said, pulling into a parking spot in front of the Starlight Café. "Do you want anything?"

Relief washed over Betty when she saw the familiar swirling letters of the sign. The dark brown building invited her in. "I'll go in with you."

"I don't have time to stay. I was just going to get it to go."

"That's fine. I just want a pastry, but I'd like to go in and see what they have." Betty was slow getting out of the car, and even though Melissa helped her, she could feel her frustration.

There was no line inside. They walked right up to the register and ordered. Betty was pleased to see a familiar face behind the counter. The young redheaded girl who had been working there for the past year took her order.

"It's nice to see you," she said to the cashier.

The cashier smiled brightly. "Thanks. It's nice to see you too." She put a croissant in a paper bag for Betty.

Looking around the café, Betty was happy to see that it looked just like it should have. Regular customers who she recognized sat at the tables. She wished the rest of her life was as familiar as this place.

With their orders in hand, she and Melissa left the café just in time to see Connie rushing up the sidewalk. "Good to see you, Betty," she said as she passed.

"Nice seeing you too," Betty said, but she wanted to reach out and catch hold of her arm. She wanted to beg her for help but knew she couldn't help her. No one could. She could only make this world right again by going back to sleep and dreaming it away.

*

Betty welcomed the fatigue that washed over her as soon as she stepped through the front door. "I'm tired. I'm going to lie down."

Melissa picked up her tablet from the coffee table. "Well, I have to get back to work. Are you going to be all right here?" She held her tablet against her chest like a schoolgirl carrying her books home.

"Of course I will. Go to work and don't worry about me." Even though Betty didn't know her, she could tell Melissa cared about her.

Betty watched Melissa leave before locking the door. She wandered from room to room, looking at the family photos. They made a handsome family, but no matter how good they looked in pictures, Betty knew it wasn't meant to be. Picking up a picture of the three of them together from the mantle, she looked closely at Casey's face. The picture was on the beach, and he looked sunburned. He squinted at the camera, holding a hand above his brow to block the sunlight. Ethan and Melissa stood next to him, laughing and looking at each other against the backdrop of the dark blue water and bright blue sky.

"It was nice meeting you, but I have to go." She set the silver picture frame down and shuffled off to bed, looking forward to her dreams and setting all of this right.

Chapter Nine

SAM tried to ignore the knot in his stomach. This wasn't how you were supposed to feel before meeting your girl after so much time away at war. He was supposed to be happy. They had written to each other almost daily. Every time he got a letter from her, he expected it to be a "Dear John." It never was. Even though he soon found himself expecting that he and Betty to last forever, something still didn't feel quite right. He couldn't put his finger on what, but the feeling had started before he even left for Korea. On the last night, when they went for the walk by the water, he was happy to learn that she had broken up with Tucker, but he couldn't push away the undercurrent of sadness that pressed at him.

When the bus pulled up to the station, Sam expected Betty to be one of the people in the crowd craning their necks to see the soldiers on the bus. He joined the flow of bodies getting off the bus and looked around the crowd, hoping to see Betty's bright face among them. She wasn't there. No one was there for him, and when he realized that, the knot in his stomach grew.

Sam ducked into a pay phone outside the bus station. He called Betty first, thinking maybe she had gotten the date mixed up. When she didn't answer, he called his father at the sandwich shop. It rang five times before anyone answered.

The shop was busy. Sam heard the commotion over the other end of the line. "Dad?"

"Samuel, is that you?" His father was practically yelling over the noise.

"I came home today. I'm at the bus station, and I was wondering if you could come pick me up."

"What about your girl? I thought she was going to do that."

Sam turned around to look out over the parking lot. Most of the people he had arrived with were gone. "She didn't show up. I think she must have gotten the dates mixed up."

"I'll be right there to pick you up."

"Thanks, Pop." Sam didn't know what to expect from his father. He wouldn't have been surprised if he had told him that he'd have to hitchhike home because the shop was too busy. That was the way it had always been, him putting the shop before anything else. So, when he said he would pick Sam up, it seemed like he was saying so much more. A lump rose in Sam's throat. "See you soon."

He stood in the now empty parking lot with his Army-issued duffel bag at his side, watching the passing cars and wondering what happened to Betty. As soon as he got home, he would surprise her. If she mistakenly thought he was supposed to be getting in tomorrow, she would be surprised. He imagined how happy she would be to see him. He imagined what it would be like to have her throw her arms around him, to feel her lips against his. He couldn't wait. He was sure the uneasiness he felt about everything would melt away in her presence.

*

Milton Accounting Firm was still open by the time Sam had washed up, changed, and headed downtown. The building was new, bright and shiny like it had come from the future. Sam knew Betty worked there but didn't expect to see her as soon as he pushed open the glass doors. She sat at the desk in the front wearing a pale green blouse with a bow at the neck. The headset she wore made her look so official. Sam bounded up to the desk, but the smile he expected was not there. She frowned deeply, creases forming in her forehead, and shook her head at him as she talked into the headset. She held up a finger, telling him to wait a minute. He stood awkwardly at the desk with his hands in his pockets. Men in suits came in, all giving a nod to Betty as they passed.

When she finally hung up, she turned her attention to him. He expected her to jump off her chair, run over, and embrace him, but she sat calmly. "I'm back. Aren't you going to kiss me?" He walked around to the other side of the desk.

She stood and he kissed her. She kissed him back, but there was something wrong. Her body was rigid. He could tell she was holding back. He wondered if that was because they were at her job.

"I thought you'd be happy to see me." He looked into her eyes, but she looked down and then over his shoulder at the door. "Aren't you glad to see me? I just came back from the war."

She took a step backward and smoothed down her skirt. "Of course I'm glad to see you. All I do is think about you, but...." Her voice shook, and that made him nervous.

"But what? All those letters you sent me. I thought...."

"I messed everything up." She put her hand on his chest.

"What do you mean?" He tried to hold her gaze, but she kept looking away. "Are you seeing somebody else?"

She shook her head vigorously. "I don't mean that. I mean when I broke up with Tucker before the war. I wasn't supposed to do that. I messed everything up. I changed everything. I didn't mean to."

"I don't know what you're talking about. You mean you want to get back with Tucker? You regret breaking up with him?" His mind raced. This was not what he thought it was going to be. Did she still love Tucker?

She shook her head again. "I don't still love Tucker. I mean... I don't know what I mean. I just want everything to go back to the way it was." She wouldn't look at him. He didn't understand why.

"What do you mean, the way it was? I thought things were going to be getting pretty good from here on out, now that I'm back." Suddenly his head hurt. "You and me, we've got a future together, Betty. I know it." He didn't really know it. He didn't really know anything, and the uneasiness was still rising in him.

"I know we do. We definitely do, but it has to happen in a very particular way. Otherwise, everything is all wrong."

"What do you mean? It's already happened. Everything's already happened. You can't go back and change it."

"I love you, Sam. I really do, but I have to make things right with Tucker. I've been thinking about it, and that's the only way I can fix what needs to be fixed."

"I don't understand. If you love me, why would you go back to Tucker? If you love me, then you and I are meant to be together. That's the way it works." He looked around the lobby, wondering what the others in the room could hear. He knew his voice was getting loud, echoing off the tile floors. A group of people gathered in the corner stopped their conversation and stared at them.

"I can't explain. You have to trust me. I'm trying to get the best possible future for us. I think this is the way." She looked right at him, her large blue eyes catching hold of his and not letting go. They were pleading to be believed. He wanted to believe her, but what she said didn't make any sense. It all felt like a cruel joke.

Anger crawled through his gut. It had come more quickly than ever since the war. He wanted to lash out. He could picture himself picking up a chair and throwing it through the glass window or screaming at the top of his lungs and breaking her desk. Only in his imagination though, he could never do that in real life.

"Fine. Go back to Tucker, then. I didn't mean anything I wrote to you anyway." The last sentence was to protect his heart that was already gaping and screaming with anger.

Sam turned on his heels like a soldier and marched out of the office. He didn't punch a wall or kick the door or yell at the top of his lungs. He was in control. He was calm and cool, just like she was, even though his future was melting away.

Chapter Ten

BETTY woke up in someone else's room with a longing in her chest that made her soul ache. The walls were painted a cheery yellow. She sat up and looked around her. This place was smaller than her room. A brown area rug lay over the white tile. Her bed was scooted up against the wall in the corner. On one side was a bedside table with a white ceramic lamp on it and a dusty white lampshade. A partially filled-out crossword puzzle lay next to the lamp, folded neatly in half.

"What have I done now, Sam?" she asked the empty room. She felt the weight of a hand on her back and a reassuring warmth spread through her.

Somewhere down the hall, people were laughing. Betty took the robe from the hook on the back of the door, grabbed her cane from the doorknob, and started down the hall, anxious to see what her life had become. Unlike the hallway in her old room, this hallway led to a living room decorated in pastels and florals. The living room was open to the kitchen where a group of strangers moved around chaotically, pouring bowls of cereal and talking.

"Mom, you're up." A chestnut-haired woman in a white T-shirt and denim shorts walked toward her. Her hair was graying at the temples. "Good morning." She gave Betty a kiss on the cheek. "Everyone's having cereal, but I can make you something if you want. I'm just happy to see you up and about. You haven't been feeling well for so long."

Betty leaned her weight on her cane, trying to steady herself. Her mind was swimming. "Where's Ethan?" She had no idea where she'd woken up and who these people were, but Ethan was the constant the last time this happened. She peered over at the four young men pouring milk into cereal bowls. They all had dark hair cut at various lengths, their heights like Russian nesting dolls.

"Who?" The woman cocked her head and squinted. "Are you feeling all right, Mother?"

Betty swallowed hard. Perspiration beaded on her forehead. Her robe was too hot. "Ethan, my son, your husband. Where is he?"

The young men in the kitchen all froze. They looked over at her, brown eyes open wide. The woman took a step forward and latched onto Betty's arm. "Why don't you sit down on the sofa for a minute." She led Betty to the sky-blue sofa that was covered in pink flowers. "You had quite a fall the other day. We're all shocked that you didn't break anything. I know you're looking forward to meeting your friends to play cards, but I think you need a few more days to recover."

She settled into the sofa next to Betty and looked deeply into her eyes. Her own eyes were brown with flecks of green. "My husband, your son-in-law, Mitch, had to go to work early. There is no Ethan." The woman laughed a bit. "I mean, there is an Ethan somewhere, but certainly not in this family."

Betty took a deep, wheezing breath and then tried to take another, but no air would go in. How could it be that her only son did not exist? Who was this woman sitting next to her? She didn't want to ask because she didn't want to appear any crazier than she already did.

"Mom, are you all right?" The woman's voice was loud, as if she thought Betty couldn't hear.

While panicking to get air, she managed to nod but couldn't speak.

"Tim," the woman called to the oldest boy in the kitchen. "I have to take your grandmother to the hospital. Make sure your brothers get to school."

The boy nodded, his long hair flopping to and fro as he did. "Is Grandma all right?"

"Everything will be fine." The tension in the woman's voice said otherwise.

Once the woman got Betty into the car and they started up the road to the hospital, she made a phone call to explain to her boss why she'd be late to work. Betty had managed to calm her breathing now, but sorrow had opened up inside of her--dark, damp, and consuming. Where was Ethan? She'd raised him. She had given birth to him. He was too small and fragile and had to stay in the hospital longer than most. She still remembered the weight of his little body in her arms the first time she held him. How much he squirmed even when he was weak. The time he ran away from home because she hugged and kissed him too much. How he fell and skinned his knee so badly that the scar remained even as an adult. He was her little boy, and he existed. This woman sitting next to her meant nothing to her.

"Who are you?"

The woman had gotten off the phone, and they sat at a red light. She looked at Betty, her eyes welling with tears. "When Dr. Lee said this would happen, I didn't want to believe it." She wiped the tears from her eyes with her hand.

Then she reached out and squeezed Betty's shoulder. "Sorry, Mom. I'm trying to hold all of it together, but it's hard."

Betty studied her face. It looked so familiar, like someone she knew.

"I'm your daughter, Sharon. Don't you remember me?" The light turned green, and Sharon eased her foot onto the accelerator. They glided across the intersection in her white station wagon.

Betty's heart fluttered. She'd always wanted a daughter, but after Ethan was born, they had such a hard time getting pregnant again. She had had several miscarriages. She would never replace Ethan with someone else though.

"Sharon." She thought about the name for a little while. It was never a name she had imagined giving to a child. Then she remembered. "Are you named after anyone?"

"I was named after my grandmother. You know that already, you just have to think about it a bit." She made the left-hand turn into the hospital parking lot. "I should get you out here at the door."

"There's no need for that," Betty said. "My brain's broken, but my legs are working just fine." Betty was only starting to feel broken. Before all of this, she was as mentally sharp as anyone could be. That was quickly slipping away.

They were lucky to find a parking space close to the emergency room door. Sharon backed into the space more quickly than Betty ever could have, then got out and went around to the passenger side to help Betty out. Her hands were firm and her arms strong as she pulled Betty from the car. She stood holding her arm as Betty steadied herself on her cane.

"How is your father?" she asked.

Sharon sighed. "Dad died five years ago."

Betty took a few deep breaths. Just to be sure, she asked

the next question, even though she knew the answer. "Who is your father?"

Sharon blinked a few times. "Tucker Anderson."

*

The emergency room was not where she wanted to be. The chairs were hard, uncomfortable plastic seats that were molded to fit a body much bigger than hers. Betty sat with her hands in her lap, waiting for her name to be called. She could feel Sharon staring at her. She wanted desperately to ask more questions but was afraid of causing too much of a scene in the hospital waiting room. Every time she thought of the idea of marrying Tucker Anderson instead of Sam, she felt like she might cry. How could she have done such a thing? She couldn't work out what could've gone wrong in the past to make this happen. Tucker Anderson was never the love of her life. Sam was.

The hospital visit was the same as any hospital visit. They poked and prodded her and asked her useless questions. When they were done, they told her to make an appointment with her primary care physician and to go home and get some rest. That was the part Betty wanted to hear because she desperately wanted to go back to sleep.

"Did your father and I have a happy marriage?" Betty asked in the car on the way home.

Sharon laughed heartily. "No. You got divorced when I was seven. Nobody was getting divorced back then, so it must've been pretty terrible."

Betty felt oddly relieved at the news.

"It was a traumatic time, but looking back, I'm glad it happened. If you never divorced Dad, you never would've married Sam. You were so happy when you married Sam. He was the love of your life."

Betty put her hand over her heart and breathed a sigh of relief. "But Sam died?"

"We all do eventually. Some sooner than others." The car zipped through traffic. "Sam was great. He always treated me like his own. When Sam got sick, that's when you and Dad started speaking again. I think it worried him that you had to go through that kind of loss alone. Besides, he had remarried already and was more in love than he had ever been."

Tucker had his moments of sweetness. Betty knew that, even though he tried to be a tough jock, underneath he had a squishy center. "That was nice of him."

"It was."

*

Sharon stayed home from work, even though Betty told her she didn't have to. "The house needs a deep cleaning. I might as well do it now." She moved from room to room, carrying a yellow plastic caddy of cleaning supplies. She left each room smelling of orange peels and vinegar.

Betty went to her bedroom to try to sleep. She wanted desperately to reenter the world of dreams and begin to tinker with the past again. She hadn't been in her room long when she heard the phone ringing. It came from the small black leather purse on the wooden chair that doubled as a nightstand next to her bed. She opened it and pulled the phone out, answering it just before it stopped ringing.

"Hello?"

"Betty, it's Pat." Pat sounded just the same as she always had. "Sharon told us you won't be able to come to the Starlight Café today to play cards. You're still feeling under the weather?"

Betty nodded, even though she knew Pat couldn't see that over the phone. "I seem to have a little bit of a problem with my memory."

"I'm so sorry to hear that." Pat's voice had gotten noticeably softer. "I would hate for...."

"For what?"

"Since you can't come meet us, we were thinking that maybe we could come visit you. If you're up to it, we could even play some cards."

Betty wasn't tired yet, and she needed to see a familiar face. She and Pat had been friends for so long that she hoped seeing her would snap the present into where it needed to be. "That would be nice."

*

Her friends walked into the house slowly, as if the speed at which they moved somehow affected her memory.

"Don't dillydally. Come on in," Betty said. Happiness washed over her at the sight of her old friends.

They all settled in the living room. Sharon brought out a pitcher of iced tea and a plate of cookies for the women to help themselves to.

"You're such a marvelous hostess," Lydia said. "My own daughter could learn from you. She never offers company anything. She certainly didn't learn that from me."

They all nodded in agreement.

Sharon excused herself, saying she had some chores to get done before leaving the women to themselves.

They were all the same as they had always been. Betty remembered each and every one, their names and how they met. They sat around the living room, laughing like teenage girls and reminiscing about the past. Sharon popped in and out of the room, checking on them like an adult supervising a teenage party. They cackled with laughter.

The scene was curious to Betty. How could her life change so much and yet so little? Even though she had married Tucker and had his daughter, somehow, she was still playing cards every week with the same group of friends. Lydia was dating a new man and had taken up yoga. Dorothy had started volunteering in the local thrift store at the cash register. She said it was fun to work again and that she got special deals on clothes. Pat didn't say much of anything. She sat in the green La-Z-Boy and watched Betty, as if trying to identify the sickness in her.

"How's Bernie?" Betty finally asked. She wondered if he was sick in this version of reality too.

Pat shook her head and looked down for a moment. Then she made eye contact with Betty and said, "He has his good days and his bad days. We all do."

"Does he still know who you are?"

"Sometimes he does and sometimes he doesn't. Most of the time he doesn't anymore." Her voice had weight. "Sharon says you've been forgetting things too."

"It's not that bad. I think it's just because I bumped my head the other day." There was still a knot on the back of Betty's head, even though she didn't remember the fall.

"That's probably what it is," Lydia said. "Nothing to worry about at all."

Betty wanted to agree, but there was something to worry about. She needed to find the present, her present, the one that was right, the one that all her memories came from. Even though her friends were the same here, nothing else was, and she needed to get out. She nearly told them about what was happening to her. At one point, she'd opened her mouth to confess everything, but her throat tightened, and nothing came out.

"Are you okay?" Dorothy asked her. "You look like you're having a spell."

Betty cleared her throat. "I guess I'm getting a bit tired." They hadn't been visiting long, but Betty was starting to feel sleepy. Her top lids wanted to sink down to meet the lower ones.

"We should leave," Lydia said. "You need your rest."

With that, they all got up. Sharon appeared in the room as if on cue to say goodbye. Once they left, she helped Betty to her room.

"Maybe I should read you a bedtime story," Sharon joked as she put Betty in bed.

Betty smiled. "There's no need for that. I'll be asleep before you finish the first sentence."

It took her seconds to fall asleep.

Seconds to go back in time.

Chapter Eleven

HE didn't have to see her face to know it was Betty. She stood a few yards in front of him at the corner, waiting for the light to change. A black pencil skirt hugged her hips. Her hair was twisted atop her head, showing off her long, slender neck. Sam stopped in his tracks when he saw her. His feet stilled as if frozen to the ground, his body tensed. He hadn't seen her since she broke up with him. He'd heard that she'd gone back to Tucker, but he didn't want to believe it. Not talking to her was a way of avoiding knowing the truth.

Sam was considering turning and going the other way when for some reason Betty turned around and saw him. Her blue eyes widened with surprise, and her mouth broke into a smile. She pivoted and walked toward him with a determined stride. Sam wanted to turn and run away, but he had fought in a war and would not allow himself to run from a woman.

"Sam!" She raised her hand high above her head and waved.

"Betty, imagine running into you here." Sam kept his voice flat and emotionless. He fought his urge to walk away and instead walked toward her, a strained smile playing across his face. "Whatever have you been up to?"

"I've been looking for you." There was an urgency in her voice.

He caught himself starting to get lost in the memories of being with her. He straightened up and hardened his stance. "Why? You made it clear when you broke up with me that you didn't think we were meant to be together. What would you want with me now?"

She was still walking toward him at a steady clip, and when she stopped, her face was so close to his. Her breath was minty, her lips red and soft. "That's not what I said at all. I just told you that I needed a little more time with Tucker, that's all. We were always meant to be together."

"You don't act like it." Sam turned to walk away from her. He walked up the street quickly, hoping to reach the corner before the traffic light changed again. He could hear her heels clipping on the sidewalk as she ran after him.

"I'm sorry. I was wrong. I keep messing everything up. I want to fix it. That's what I'm trying to do. That's why I broke up with you, but that was the wrong choice. You have to be patient with me. You have to understand."

He tried to ignore her, but she had the type of voice that he couldn't block out. He heard every word but chose not to react.

"I love you, Sam. I love you more than anything."

It was as if the words repeated on a loop. They broke through every sound around him: the passing traffic, conversations, a dog barking, an airplane flying overhead. The words shattered every other sound. They stabbed him. Inside he wanted to whirl around and yell at her.

"Sam, look at me. You can't keep walking away. You are my destiny." She yelled the last sentence like a madwoman. The people on the street stared at her, then shot glances at Sam.

He whirled around. "If you love me, you have a funny way of showing it."

She stopped just short of crashing into him. "I'm trying to do what's right, but it's been harder than I thought."

He cocked his head at her. "Most people treat the person they love with respect. They want to be with them. They don't ditch them at the bus station when they're coming home from war. They don't write love letters to them every day and then break up with them as soon as they get home."

"You don't understand."

"I understand." He pointed his finger at her chest. "I understand that you are a crazy person, and I'd be just as crazy as you if I believed a word you said."

Sam turned around and walked away before she could say anything. He wasn't going to let her hurt him again. He wouldn't fall for her story about them belonging together again. She'd told him all of that before, and he got too wrapped up in the idea. He took their future for granted when nothing was set in stone. There was no way anything could be. Life was fluid. People made choices, and those choices shaped their futures, not some predetermined destiny. He knew that now and was determined to shape his own future and not let her manipulate it.

Sam quickened his steps until he was practically running. He weaved through the cars to cross the street against the light, horns blaring at him in anger. He ran all the way home without so much as checking over his shoulder to see if she was following him. Walking up the porch steps, he pulled the key from his pants pocket and turned around, looking for her, half expecting to see her right behind him. She wasn't there. The sidewalk was empty. Still, he slipped inside quickly, just in case she was right around the corner.

The knock on the door was so light that it was barely

audible. Sam and his father sat at the kitchen table talking, and at first, they weren't sure if they had heard a knock at all.

"Did you hear something?" Sam's father asked, looking up at the door.

The war had damaged Sam's hearing, not enough to affect his communication, but enough to mask the tiny sounds around him. He shrugged. The knock happened again, that time a bit louder.

Sam's father got up and walked to the door. His hair was almost completely gray now, and he walked with a limp, the result of a car accident he was in when Sam was away. He opened the door just a crack. Sam turned around in his seat, watching to see who it might be. His father talked for a little while before finally opening the door all the way and letting the guest in.

She still lit up the room. Betty had changed into a pair of pedal pushers and a short-sleeve gingham button-up shirt. Her hair was pulled up into a high ponytail.

Sam couldn't help but gaze at her longingly, before he remembered he was angry. He rocketed up out of his seat and started for the back door when he felt his father's firm hand on his shoulder.

"She wants to talk to you. You should give her a chance." His steely eyes drove into Sam.

"I already did. Why should I trust her again?" His words were pointed. He spoke loudly, wanting to make sure she heard.

She was quiet as she sat on the edge of the sofa, leaning forward slightly like she would get up at any moment.

Sam's father looked behind him, as if checking to see if she could hear their conversation. There was no doubt she could; there was only a thin wall and an open doorway between them. He looked back at Sam and lowered his head, as if doing so would make his voice quieter. "She's a pretty good girl. To be honest, if you ended up with her, you'd be doing better than I ever thought you would."

Sam tensed under the sting of the words but remained quiet.

"She came all the way over here because she had something to say to you. The least you can do is go in there and let her say it. It'll take a few minutes of your time. I don't want to have to explain why you ran out the back door like a coward." He grabbed a pack of cigarettes from the kitchen table. "I'm going to go out back for a smoke and give you guys the privacy you need." He stood, squarely looking at Sam, waiting for him to step out of the way. "You want to let me through?"

Sam stepped aside.

His father brushed past him, pushing the door open. Before he stepped outside, he turned back to Sam and said, "Just listen to her for a few minutes. That's all I ask."

His father asking was enough to make Sam not want to do it at all. Sam slid him a sidelong glance as he stepped outside. He thought seriously about leaving. Even though he still lived in his father's house, he was a grown man and didn't have to follow his rules.

From where he stood, he could only see Betty from the knees down. Her legs were pressed together. Her feet, encased in pink ballerina flats, bounced nervously. He tried desperately to hate her, but if he was honest with himself, he could never do that. He always wanted to hear what she had to say.

Sam bit his lip and ran his fingers through his dark brown hair. He inhaled, puffing up his chest and pulling back his shoulders, then let out a long, slow breath. He took the first step and then the next across the mustard-yellow linoleum floor to the living room.

Her whole form revealed itself to him before he passed through the arched door of the kitchen. Arms crossed, she looked up at him with pleading eyes. She didn't hold his gaze long before looking away. Her legs stilled, and she uncrossed her arms. "I was afraid you wouldn't see me."

Sam wanted to see her every day forever. He wanted to hear her voice all the time, but the sweetness of her presence had been replaced with the ragged edge of pain. He wished everything would go back to the way it was. If he could go back in time, he would go back to the day he got off the bus and he would change things. She would be there waiting for him.

But he couldn't go back in time. There were consequences for what had happened.

"Here I am. Say what you have to say." He didn't want her to know that he cared. He shoved his pain deep down inside.

She bit the inside of her cheek, lines forming in her forehead.

"You came all the way over here. You must have something to say." He liked the advantage standing over her seemed to give him. He told himself that there was no way she could hurt him again if he kept towering over her like this.

"What if I told you that I've seen our future? We have a son named Ethan. We live in a nice house."

"You're not allowed to do that. You can't create a future for us based on something you can't even commit to." Sam walked to the front door and pulled it open. "I don't have time for this nonsense. You should go home."

She wasn't done talking yet. She remained anchored to the couch. "The first time I came back, I wanted to change things, so we could have more time together because you are my heart, and I lost you too soon." Her voice broke, and she sniffled. She pulled a tissue from her pocket and wiped her nose. "But when I went back to the present, I realized I changed everything about our lives by breaking up with Tucker and dating you too soon. So, I came back here again, and I tried to fix it."

She blew her nose again. "Then I went back, and it was all wrong because you weren't in my life at all. I'm trying to make this right. You are my heart. You're the man I'm supposed to be with. I'm trying to fix it so the present--" She shook her head. "I mean the future can be the one I remember. I'm tired of waking up and finding everything in my life wrong." Her voice quivered.

Sam fought the urge to comfort her. "What you're saying is madness. What's happened to you since I've been gone?"

"I'm the same girl. The girl from the ice cream store. I just know a little more." A tear slid down her face.

"I don't know what to say, Betty. I think you need help. Does Tucker know you think you can travel through time?"

"You're all caught up in the traveling through time and missing the most important part." She stood up, walked around the coffee table, and stopped in front of him. "We're meant to be together."

"Have you told Tucker that too?" He hated saying Tucker's name, but he was trying to make a point.

"When are you going to realize that it doesn't matter what Tucker knows? What matters is what you know."

"I know you didn't show up for me when I came back from fighting the commies in Korea. I know you told me you wanted to go back to your old boyfriend. I know what you're saying right now is craziness and you need to get some help. You can't get it here. I can't help you. You need to go somewhere where someone can help you get in touch with reality. People don't travel through time. That doesn't happen.

It probably never will. Stop wasting my time and go home to your boyfriend."

As he spoke, he circled her, and when he got into the right position, he stepped toward her again and again, making her step back until she was out the front door and standing on the patio. He ended his speech by closing the door in her face. He expected the act to feel good, but it didn't. It was almost like cutting off a limb.

Sam stood silent and still, listening, hoping to hear her shoes walking down the creaky wooden steps. He heard nothing. He pictured her still standing there, mosquitoes swarming her, attracted to her gardenia perfume.

He stood listening for what felt like hours. Then he heard the slow creak of one step and then another. He went to the window where he could watch her walking slowly up the street. She twisted and looked back at the house three times before disappearing around the corner.

Chapter Twelve

DISAPPOINTMENT overwhelmed Betty when she opened her eyes. She rolled over onto her back and looked at the white ceiling. "No, no." A tear slid across her temple and into her hair. "I don't understand."

Betty didn't want to get up, not in the same reality she had gone to bed in. She tried so hard to fix it and hadn't been successful. She lay on her back, thinking about her dream and trying to figure out what she could do next time to make Sam believe her and change his mind.

She couldn't remember how many scenarios she had run through her head when there was a light knocking on her door. The sun had sunk lower in the sky.

"Mom, are you all right?" Sharon pushed the door open a crack and peered in.

Betty used the edge of her sheet to dry her eyes. Her bedroom felt completely empty. Not even a hint of Sam lingered in the space around her. She hadn't felt so alone in years.

Sharon rushed in. "Are you okay? Are you in pain?"

"I'm not in any more pain than I usually am." She turned on her side and pushed herself up. The lower ribs on her right side throbbed.

Sharon reached down and supported her shoulder to help her. "Why are you crying?"

"I just had a bad dream."

"It must've been pretty terrible." Sharon sat on the bed and put her hand on Betty's back.

She looked at the bedside table, expecting to see what she saw before, a picture of Sharon's family--her four sons and her husband next to a picture of Betty and Sam at the Grand Canyon--but the picture of Betty and Sam was missing. In its place sat a picture of Betty and Tucker at Niagara Falls. "What happened to the other picture that used to be here?"

Sharon looked at the bedside table for a moment. "What other picture?"

"The picture of me and Sam at the Grand Canyon. Someone's put this here instead." She held up the photo of her and Tucker and shook it.

"That was yours and Dad's best vacation. You love that picture. I do too because you look like you're so much in love."

Betty looked at the picture again. She didn't see any love there. She smiled, but there was an emptiness in her eyes. "Where's the picture of me and Sam?"

"Mom, I don't know who Sam is."

Betty was lucky she was sitting down, because she was sure if she hadn't been, she would've passed out. "What do you mean, you don't know who Sam is? He's the man I married after your father, and I got divorced."

That look was back again, the same one Sharon had given her when she got up that morning. Her face scrunched. "You and Dad never got divorced. You certainly never married anyone named Sam."

Betty's heart slammed against her chest. "That can't be

right. That can't be right."

"I'm going to call the doctor again. Obviously, there's still something wrong here. I'll see if we can have you put in the hospital for observation or something." Sharon got up and walked toward the door.

"Sharon, I'm not crazy. I'm fine."

"You're obviously having a problem with your memory. We have to get this taken care of. If they know what it is, maybe they can give you some kind of medication to slow it down at least. Stay in bed and rest."

"Don't call the doctor. I don't need to go back to the hospital. I was just confused for a minute. I'm fine now."

Holding the doorknob, Sharon turned to look at her. "Are you sure?"

Betty nodded. "I'm so fine that I think I'm going to get up in a minute."

"Okay," Sharon said. "Do you need help getting out of bed?"

Betty shook her head. "I said I'm fine. I'll be out in a minute."

Sharon left the door open a crack when she left.

Betty didn't think she could sleep any more than she already had. She was restless and had to go to the bathroom, but getting up would mean that everything Sharon had said was true. If she sat up and put her feet on the floor, she would be grounded in this new reality, a reality she did not want.

She picked up the picture of the Niagara Falls vacation. In it she and Tucker stood in front of the falls in electric blue ponchos. The rushing water was a mixture of gray and white foam. Tucker smiled so wide that his eyes were slits. She smiled too, but it was forced. It didn't reach her eyes like it should have. She wondered how her daughter didn't seem to notice.

Betty laid the photo face down on the table, not wanting to look at it. She wanted to wish it out of existence. She wanted to wish this whole version of reality out of existence.

When her bare feet hit the rough carpet, it almost hurt. Tears ran down her face. She reached for a tissue from the bedside table to blot her eyes. How could she have gotten it so wrong?

She picked up her cane, her hip groaning as she walked through the living room to the bathroom. Sharon stood by the front door, flipping through a stack of mail.

"I'm glad you decided to get up." Noticing Betty wincing as she walked, Sharon put the mail down and rushed over, grabbing her arm.

"I'm okay. I just need to walk it off." She was too unsteady on her feet to pull away.

"Your hip seems to be getting worse. Maybe we should think about replacing that cane with a walker."

Betty shook her head. "I don't need a walker. The cane is fine. I really have to use the little girl's room." She shuffled into the bathroom with Sharon still at her side. The tile was cold and hard. She flipped on the bright light and turned to Sharon. "I can still handle this on my own."

"I know. I just don't want you to fall." Sharon let go of her arm and looked around the cramped space. "I'm sorry. Go ahead and do your business. I'll be out here if you need anything." She pointed out of the bathroom door.

Betty gave a little nod. "Okay then." They looked at each other for a few moments. "I still have to pee."

"Right, sorry." She looked a bit flustered before finally stepping out the door and closing it behind her.

Sharon was standing in front of the bathroom door with her arms crossed when Betty came out. "I can't believe you really waited out here."

Sharon shrugged and looked at the floor. Her light brown eyes were glossy. "I just don't know what to do, Mom. I wanted to make sure I could get in there quickly if something went wrong."

"Don't fret. Everything came out okay." Betty chuckled.

Sharon didn't laugh though. She began to sob, her shoulders shaking and her breath hitching.

Betty hobbled toward her. "Honey, don't cry. I just had to use the bathroom."

"You know what I'm crying about." She hiccupped in the middle of her sentence. "I'm afraid I'm losing you."

"You're not losing me. I'm right here." Betty could see Tucker so clearly in Sharon's face. The honey-colored eyes, dark hair, square jawline, and strong chin made her a handsome woman. Everything about her was square like Tucker. She had a dimple on her left cheek that was there whether she was laughing or not.

Noticing Betty staring at her, she wiped her tears. "What?"

Betty shook her head. "Nothing. You look so much like your father."

"You always say that. It's good because I feel like I have a piece of him with me all the time."

Betty had been so caught up in her own problems that she never really thought about how her appearances in these alternate realities affected her family. She never intended to marry Tucker or have children with him, but he was still Sharon's father. She wondered how long ago he died, but realized asking would cause more pain than she wanted. "You do. You always have a piece of him with you. You always have a piece of me with you too."

Sharon hugged her so gently, it was as if she thought she might break.

"I have an idea," Betty said. "Let's go get some coffee and

a pastry. My treat."

Sharon looked at her watch.

"Unless you have someplace to go...."

"No. Coffee sounds like a great idea."

"Let's go to the Starlight Café?" Betty wasn't even sure if the café existed in this version of reality.

"Is there anywhere else we would go?"

*

Betty ached for something familiar, and the Starlight Café did not disappoint. When she stepped inside, she was relieved to see that it looked the way it always had: the white tile floors, dark wooden bar, and matching tables and chairs all neatly lined up. She wondered if she would see anyone familiar there.

Betty found the table while Sharon waited in line to order. She scanned the faces of the other customers, looking for someone she knew, but no one was familiar. Then she saw the owner, Connie, come out of the back room. She stood behind the coffee bar surveying the café. Her full cheeks were rosy, and sweat beaded her brow like she had been doing some kind of hard labor. When she looked in Betty's direction, Betty waved. Connie came out from behind the bar and bounced over to her.

"It's been a while. I'm glad to see you're feeling better," she chirped.

"It hasn't been that long, has it?" Betty had just been there a week ago playing cards with her girlfriends.

"It's been a few months. Your crew really misses you."

Betty's thoughts darted back and forth like dragonflies. How could it be? "They still come here every week? The same women?"

Connie cocked her head at Betty. A questioning look passed over her face before she answered. "Of course, but the group isn't the same without you." Connie looked around the café. "Are you here alone today?"

"Sharon is here. She's in line."

"A mother-daughter day out. That sounds nice."

Betty smiled, even though she didn't think of Sharon as her daughter. She looked over at her waiting in line, her hands shoved into the pockets of her denim shorts. Wispy flyaways had escaped her ponytail. She examined the pastries in the dessert case as she waited. Betty wondered what she was like as a child. Even though this perversion of her life was not the correct version, she was curious about what it would've been like to raise a girl. She wondered what Tucker was like as a husband.

"I'm living somebody else's life."

The sound of the chair legs scraping on the floor brought Betty's attention back to Connie, who was sitting down at the table across from her now. "I used to feel like that too. I was a lot younger then."

"I guess you're saying I'm a little late coming to this conclusion." She sat back in her chair and grabbed hold of her cane. She enjoyed the comfort of holding on to it. It was the only familiar thing that she had brought with her through her alternate realities.

"It's never too late to realize what you want."

"Even if what you want is already long gone?" Betty felt hot behind the eyes but was determined not to cry again.

"What do you mean by that?" Connie, who was normally quite a brash woman, managed to speak to Betty in a gentle tone.

"I feel like I let the love of my life get away."

"That's a sad thing to realize now."

Betty looked down at her hand gripping the handle of the cane. Her fingers were slender, but her joints had become knobby and rounded. "Especially since he's already dead and gone." She reached into her pants pocket and pulled out a tissue to wipe her nose.

Connie sucked her teeth. "That really is sad."

"You haven't even heard the saddest part. I was trying to fix everything so we could spend more time together, but in the midst of all my fixing, I ended up losing them altogether." Betty wished she could control where she went back to in her dreams. If she could, she would've set it all right by having time play out like it was supposed to. She was foolish to think she could manipulate her own destiny.

"The love of my life left me for something he loved more," Connie shared. "I thought the heartbreak would kill me at the time, but I'm here. I'm stronger for it. I try to remind myself to be happy for the memories of the good times that we had together. Of course, they weren't always the best, but when it was good, it was incredibly good." Her eyes sparkled when she spoke.

"You do have a point." Even though Betty was living a different life than she intended, somehow, she still had the memory of Sam and what they had together. That had never gone away.

Sharon came over carrying a piece of carrot cake and a croissant. She said hello to Connie as she put the plate on the table. "I'll be right back with the coffee." She stood at the bar, adding sugar to Betty's drink. Betty watched her carefully as she put the exact right amount of sugar in.

"You got a good daughter there." Connie stood.

"She does seem to treat me well, doesn't she?"

"Certainly does." Connie looked around the café again. The girl behind the register called something to her, and

Connie gave her a nod. "I'll leave you ladies in peace to enjoy your coffee. It was good seeing you again, Betty." She left as Sharon was putting the coffee on the table.

"Connie's always so friendly," Sharon said. "That's one of the reasons I like this place."

"Connie said they still meet for cards here on Monday."

Sharon took a bite of her cake and nodded. "Pat, Lydia, and Dorothy all came by to visit you just last week. You know they still come here and play cards. Don't you remember?"

Knowing how much her memory loss had upset Sharon, Betty pretended she remembered. "Of course."

"You're probably feeling well enough to start playing with them again."

Betty wondered if it was the caffeine and sugar making Sharon so optimistic. When she had taken her to the doctor, it seemed like Sharon thought Betty was dying. Betty felt like she was dying. Realizing she might've messed things up so badly that she had erased Ethan completely made her heart ache. "That would be nice. Maybe I should call Pat when I get home."

"That's a good idea. She would love to hear from you."

Betty's croissant was perfect. She drank her coffee quickly, hoping it would keep her awake a little while longer. With the way her dream turned out last time, she decided she needed a little time to plan before she went to sleep again. She needed to come up with the best way to win Sam over.

Chapter Thirteen

BETTY spent a good fifteen minutes in her room looking for her cell phone before she finally gave up. She went out into the living room where Sharon sat on the couch reading a book. "I can't find my cell phone anywhere."

Sharon closed her book, leaving her thumb to hold her place. "You never had a cell phone."

"How can I call you if I have a problem while I'm out?"

"You don't go out that much. You only go to the coffee shop once a week, and if something happens, you use one of your friends' phones. That's only happened once though." Betty could tell by the way Sharon pulled her eyebrows together that she was worrying again.

"Right. I just forgot for a minute. Don't worry about it. Everything's fine." She turned and walked back to her room, putting all her weight on her cane.

"Don't you want the phone so you can call Pat?" Sharon took the phone off the cradle on the table next to the sofa. She set her book down on the cushion next to her and walked over to Betty.

"Thanks. I almost forgot."

Betty shut her bedroom door and sat on her bed. This

whole situation might have made some people think her brain was turning into Swiss cheese, but in reality, Betty had always been very sharp. She dialed Pat's number right away. She had committed it to memory years ago. Pat answered on the second ring.

"Pat? It's me, Betty."

"Betty, it's so good to hear your voice. How are you doing? Are you still on the mend? You were looking so good when we were there the other day." Pat's voice was unusually cheery.

"I'm doing well. I've been forgetting a few things, or at least it looks like I've been forgetting a few things, but I don't really think I am. Or maybe I'm forgetting a few things and I've forgotten that I've forgotten."

Pat laughed.

Betty laughed too. It was good that someone else saw how ridiculous her predicament was, even if she really didn't understand.

"Hopefully you won't forget how to play cards."

"I'll never forget that." Betty pursed her lips. She hadn't planned on asking Pat about Sam, but now that she had her on the phone... "Do you remember Sam?"

"It's been a while since you've talked about him." Her voice bubbled. "I never understood why you left him for Tucker in the first place. The whole time he was at war, you were head over heels in love with him. From what you showed me of his letters, he felt the same way about you."

"I was stupid back then."

"We all were."

Talking to someone who knew about her and Sam made Betty feel like she was on firm ground again. She wasn't crazy. "I wonder what happened to him."

"You say that like you don't already know."

This intrigued Betty. "What do you mean?"

"You know what I mean," she whispered, and Betty had to strain to hear her. "Don't make me spell it out for you. You made me promise never to tell anyone."

"Tell anyone what?"

"That you tracked Sam down." She was still talking in that strange whisper.

"Talk in your normal voice so I can understand you." Realizing her bedroom door was open, Betty got up and pushed it closed. "When did I track him down?" Now Betty was whispering.

"Forever ago now. Sharon was just a kid." Pat made a clucking sound. "Don't tell me you've forgotten."

"I must've. What did I find out about him?"

"Betty, I'm worried about you. Have you been to the doctor about this? What if you're getting Alzheimer's like Bernie? I really think you should see a doctor."

Betty wasn't interested in hearing about the doctor. "I've already gone. He says I'm fine."

"Maybe you should get a second opinion."

"Just tell me about Sam." She didn't mean to snap.

"Don't get short with me. I don't have to tell you anything." Pat huffed.

"I'm sorry. I've just been thinking about Sam a lot these days. I wonder about what happened to him and--"

"--how your life would be different if you would've married him instead of Tucker. That kind of thinking doesn't help anything. You know that."

"Yeah, but I keep dreaming about Sam these days. I can't seem to get him off my mind. I can't help but think there's a reason for that."

Betty remembered the slip of paper with Sam's phone number on it that had originally started this whole ordeal. She went over to her purse hanging over the chair in the corner.

Cradling the phone between her shoulder and ear to free up her hands, she opened her purse and started looking through it.

"Betty, are you still there?"

"Yeah. I'm just looking for something." She found the crumpled piece of paper in the side pocket of her purse where she kept her wallet. The large loopy letters stared back at her, reminding her of the woman she once was. She settled into the chair. "Please tell me what became of Sam. I need to know."

"Are you okay?"

"Yes. I'm fine. Tell me."

"He wasn't hard for you to find. You just did some asking around. Once his dad died, he never came back in town, but I think Kevin Beecher had kept in touch with him. Remember Kevin?"

Betty did remember Kevin. He was a lanky kid who warmed the bench during most of the basketball games. He was too clumsy to play. She always wondered how he got on the team. "Yeah, I remember him."

"He told you Sam was teaching at a university in Massachusetts. I can't remember the name of it offhand. It wasn't Harvard or anything. He ran off to Boston after you broke up with him and never came back to town. Not that I was aware of that. Who would blame him? You broke his heart. He probably moved up north because he wanted to get as far away from you as possible."

"You don't know that."

"He pretty much told you that when you went up to visit him."

"I went to visit him? What about Tucker and Sharon?"

"It's your life, Betty. I shouldn't have to tell you about it. You told him that you had found some long-lost relatives you needed to go visit because you were doing your family history or some nonsense. I remember being so angry because you made me lie to him too. You know I hate doing that."

"I know. Thank you for doing that for me." Betty searched her mind, looking for the memory of going to see Sam, but her memories were all from a different version of reality. "What happened? Did I see him?"

"It mustn't have gone very well, because when you got home you were so miserable and didn't want to talk about it. So, I don't know what happened. It's up to you to remember that."

If Sam had treated her badly, she was glad she couldn't remember, but she wished her life was her own again.

"Thank you for telling me about what happened. I appreciate it. You've always been a good friend." Betty was grateful that some things in her life remained constant no matter what choices she had made in the past.

"So have you."

"How's Bernie? I need to get over there and visit him."

"He's not well. Don't feel obligated to visit. He probably won't know who you are anyway. He doesn't remember me most days." Her voice was heavy.

"As soon as I'm well enough, I'll visit him again." Betty didn't know if she'd be able to keep that promise in this version of reality. Once she got back to her version, she would. She'd enjoyed the time she spent with him during the last visit.

"I should go," Pat said.

Talking to her had calmed Betty so much that the idea of hanging up made her anxious. Pat was the only person who made her feel sane. "Can't you talk a little bit longer?"

"I guess. I don't want to keep you though."

"You're not keeping me from anything. All I do is sit

around the house most of the time."

"You don't have to convince me. Bernie always said I was born with the phone attached to my ear."

The two spent about an hour reminiscing about high school. Betty was happy to talk about the one time in her life that seemed constant with someone.

Chapter Fourteen

SAM held a paper bag of groceries as he stood looking out the plate glass window. Rain pelted the glass. Lightning cracked the sky. The redheaded woman next to him let out a small yelp and cupped her hand over her mouth in embarrassment. "Storms always scare me," the woman said. "I guess I moved to the wrong state." She chewed on her bottom lip as she looked out the window, giving her the appearance of someone much younger.

"Don't worry. We're safe in here," Sam reassured.

The woman crossed her arms over her chest. The thunder crashed, and she jumped. "Sorry."

"There's no reason to apologize." Sam looked out at the storm, then back at the woman. "My name is Sam Hawthorne. My father owns Hawthorne Sandwiches downtown."

"I've never eaten there. I've seen it, but--" The thunder roared again, and the woman jumped. "Sorry." She brushed the hair off her face. "My name is Emily Johnston."

"Nice to meet you, Ms. Johnston."

"You can call me Emily. Is it okay if I call you Sam?"

"Of course it is." Sam was enjoying his conversation with Emily when he felt something brush his left arm. He looked to see what it was and to his annoyance found Betty standing next to him.

"I was just thinking about you, and then I find you standing here." She hoisted her grocery bag up on her hip.

"I wasn't thinking about you." He turned his attention back to the redhead who was looking at him with her mouth agape. Her upturned nose crinkled. Sam realized how rude he must've seemed. "She's an old acquaintance. We're having a bit of a disagreement, but she won't be bothering us anymore." He threw a stern glance at Betty.

"That's not quite true. I have something I need to talk to you about. I hope you don't mind, Emily, was it?" Betty leaned around Sam to talk to the woman.

"Of course not. We were just making small talk while waiting for the storm to die down." With that, Emily slunk off toward the other end of the store to look at the candy bars.

"I don't have anything to say to you." Sam shook his head as he spoke.

"You don't have to speak. Just listen."

"I think I heard enough when you told me you traveled from the future. How has time travel been treating you?" The sarcastic edge in his voice was meant to hurt.

"Forget the whole time-travel thing. I'm sorry I mentioned it. I wasn't serious." She looked around as if to check if anyone else was listening to what they were saying.

"When someone tells you they travel through time, it's pretty hard to forget."

"I was joking."

"You seemed pretty serious to me."

"I'm silly sometimes. I'm sorry you didn't get my joke."

"Were you also joking when you said you broke up with Tucker? I asked around and no one else seems to think you have."

She looked confused. Her brows knitted together, and she pursed her lips. Sam could see that she was chewing on the inside corner of her cheek. She had a habit of doing that when she was thinking. "I'm pretty sure I broke up with Tucker. Maybe he's too embarrassed to tell anyone yet. I don't know what's going on."

"You should know what's going on. It's your relationship."

"You know how Tucker is. He probably wants to make sure everyone thinks he broke up with me."

"Betty! Betty!" a sharp voice called her from across the store.

Sam and Betty looked in the direction of the voice and saw a young blonde woman waving at them. She sashayed through the crowd effortlessly.

"Alexandra, how are you?" Betty's voice dripped with honey.

"I haven't seen you in ages. It shouldn't be like that. I should see my future sister-in-law every day." Alexandra showed off a row of perfect white teeth. She beamed at Sam. "I don't think we've met. I'm Alexandra, Tucker's sister."

"I'm Sam Hawthorne." He raised an eyebrow at Betty.

At the sound of his name, Alexandra's expression soured. She looked at Betty, then at Sam, and then at Betty again. "You two are here together?"

"Yes, as a matter of fact we--"

"Aren't," Sam broke in. "We just happened to see each other because we were both waiting for the rain to stop."

Alexandra nodded but suspicion played across her face. "That's a coincidence." She looked at Betty again.

"It is."

"You must be looking forward to the wedding." Sam sneered at Betty as he spoke. He was pleased to catch her in a lie.

"Yes, we all are." Alexandra squeezed Betty's arm enthusiastically. "I can't believe my older brother's getting married to such a great girl. He's so lucky." She put emphasis on the last sentence, as if to prove something to Sam.

"Betty sure is something else," Sam said.

"She definitely is," Alexandra agreed.

The rain died almost as quickly as it had started. "I have to get going. It was nice talking to you two." Sam joined the other shoppers who had decided they were ready to brave what had now become a light drizzle and go to their cars.

The thunder still boomed in the distance. He didn't check to see if Betty had followed him. He hoped she hadn't. Sam would never admit it, but every time he saw her, the wound in his heart opened. Even though he questioned her sanity, he couldn't help but love her. But he was a logical man and couldn't abide the games she played.

He wanted a simple life. He wanted an easy-to-understand life, and he knew he would not be able to have that with Betty. What he could have with her didn't matter anyway, because it was obvious from the conversation that she had never actually broken it off with Tucker. He had to get used to that, the idea of his life without her. He was just starting to work that out, making plans to leave. That was what he would have to do to get over her.

Chapter Fifteen

THE sheets were scratchy against her legs. Betty pulled at the top one until it came untucked at the bottom. Pulling the sheet aside, she hung her right foot off the bed. Her hair stuck in the sweat on her forehead and the back of her neck.

"Are you okay? Are you awake?" The voice pressed into her, pulling her into the present.

A hand gently squeezed hers. Betty looked to her left and saw Pat sitting in the chair next to her. "I'm fine. I think I just had a bad dream."

"It's okay, honey. You're awake now. No worries," Pat cooed.

"I know." Betty looked around her room. It wasn't the same one she'd just gone to sleep in at Sharon's house. This room had white walls and beige tile floors. Narrow windows stood in a line along the far wall. An aqua chair sat next to the windows, its cushions covered in vinyl. On another wall hung a painting of a vase of flowers. It was too characterless to be anything that Betty would've picked out herself. A blond wooden door led to a darkened bathroom. Betty could only see the beginning of the small white tiles on the bathroom floor from her position on the bed. A wheeling metal tray sat beside the bed. On it was a bowl of half-eaten applesauce and a piece of cold toast on a white plate. A thick pad of butter lounged in the middle, unmelted. "Where am I?"

A worried frown appeared on Pat's face. "You're in Bayview Nursing Home. Don't you remember?"

Betty shook her head. "What am I doing here? What happened to...?" She didn't know who to ask about--Ethan, Tawana, or Sharon. She had no idea what version of the present she was in.

"Nothing happened to anyone." Pat looked over at the door. "Maybe I should call a nurse."

"No," Betty said. "I don't need a nurse. What happened to my family?"

Pat went silent. It was as if everything in the whole nursing home had stopped. Silence washed over them. Betty looked into Pat's eyes, her own eyelids twitching as she searched for answers in them.

Pat opened her mouth, but no sound came out. She clamped it closed again, then reached down and patted Betty's hand before finally saying, "You don't have a family."

Betty squeezed her eyes shut, wishing this version of the present would vanish because it was worse than any of the others she'd experienced.

"That's not possible. I married Sam... or Tucker. Either way we have a child, sometimes a boy, sometimes a girl."

Pat's gaze bounced from Betty to the door then back to Betty again. "Maybe I should call the nurse."

"What for? I'm fine. I'm fine. Everything is fine. Everything is the way it's supposed to be, which is just fine." Betty lowered her eyes to the thin blanket covering all but her right leg, which still hung out of the bed. The green fabric was woven in a raised checkered pattern. She touched the rough surface and could feel the rise of each square beneath her fingertips. "Is that why I'm here? Because I didn't have a family?"

Pat shrugged. She continued to look at the door before returning her attention to Betty. "A lot of people here have families. Sometimes your family can't take care of you the way a nurse can. Who knows if you would be here if you had a family? So, I can't say that's why you're here. You're here because you've been getting confused."

"In what way?"

"Like what happened just now. You claim you were married when you weren't. You ask about a son you never had and granddaughters who don't exist. You gave them names. We played along at first because we thought you were joking."

"Who's we?"

"You know, the girls and me. You remember them, don't you? Lydia, Dorothy."

Betty smiled calmly at the sound of the familiar names. "Yes. I remember."

"I know sometimes you regret not having a family, but making one up isn't the answer."

Betty scowled. "That's obvious, isn't it? Why would I make something like that up?"

"I'm not sure. We were never sure."

"That's how I ended up here?"

"And you fell. It all started when you fell off the stepladder in the kitchen."

Betty remembered that fall well. That was the fall that made Ethan decide she needed to move in with him. She wondered what else her realities had in common. "Do you remember the day we first met Sam at the ice cream shop?"

"How could I forget? He was so good-looking. I had a crush on him from the start, but he clearly wasn't interested in me." Her face lit up looking back on it.

"Remember how I dated him through the war? We wrote each other every day."

Pat continued to smile. "I was so shocked when you dropped Tucker like a hot potato. I was even more shocked when he took you back after all that."

So that was where this was going. "Then I dumped him for Sam again." Betty continued testing the waters. She sent her words out like feelers.

"But Sam didn't want anything to do with you, and then you had no one. When that happened, I was so shocked, but I didn't think you wouldn't end up with either one of them." That was the missing piece that Betty was looking for.

A scream echoed in the hall. Two nurses ran by Betty's open door, their hair pulled up in ponytails, their scrubs faded.

Pat stood, her wide eyes looking at the door. "I have to go. I think that's Bernie." Before Betty could say anything, Pat left her room and rushed down the hallway.

Betty lay on her adjustable bed with her head nestled in a pile of pillows, listening. Even after the struggle had ended, Pat didn't come back to visit her.

Betty flipped through television channels. She welcomed sleep when it came. Her heavy eyelids drew her into a better place than the world she was in now.

Chapter Sixteen

SAM'S father drove him to the bus station one balmy afternoon. Neither of them touched the radio. They listen to the whir of the tires on the blacktop and the engine propelling them forward. Sam watched the city passing through the passenger window. Soon he would be gone forever. He hadn't told his father that he never planned on coming back. It was hard to believe that the whole time he was in Korea, all he thought about was this place, the city, the woman who lived in it who he thought was his destiny. Life could change in the blink of an eye. That's what they always said. He didn't realize how true it was until the day he met Betty. She changed him twice, once into a man who finally believed in love, then into a man who would never trust love again.

When he pulled up in front of the bus station, Sam looked at his father, whose square jaw tensed.

"Do you need me to go inside with you?" He gripped the steering wheel and looked straight ahead when he spoke.

"No. I can manage." He planned to buy a bus ticket to Boston. A friend who served in Korea with him lived there. He had an extra room and told Sam that work in the city was easy to come by. Sam would work and go back to school. He would never think about Betty again.

The two men sat in the car in the parking lot, watching the people going to and from the bus station. Men and women together and alone hurried back and forth. Some had children. Others did not. Some dragged suitcases much too heavy to lift. Others traveled with only a small briefcase. Some had nothing at all.

Sam got out of the car without a word. His father turned off the engine and got out too. They walked around to the trunk and his father opened it. Sam hoisted his Army-issued duffel bag out of the trunk. He had packed everything he owned, which wasn't much. His father stood watching him, his back straight and his arms at his sides. He stood at attention like a soldier ready to go off to war, but he was just going home to an empty house without his wife or his son. Sam didn't worry about him because he had done fine when he was in Korea. He would do fine now. Boston wasn't that far away.

"I guess I'm off." Sam's voice cracked with emotion. He wanted to turn away from his father and hide the tears he felt welling in his eyes. When he'd made this plan, he didn't think leaving would be hard. He was only thinking about getting away from Betty and didn't fully consider what it might feel like to leave his father. They were never close. It shouldn't have mattered. But this time it seemed to matter even more than when he went to Korea. When he went to Korea, he knew that, if he lived, he would be back. Now he was pretty sure he would never return.

"Be safe," his father said.

Sam thought he heard his father's voice quiver, but later he would convince himself otherwise. He had a knack for hearing only what he wanted.

They didn't hug. His father didn't say, "I love you, son,"

and he didn't say, "I love you, Dad." That wasn't the way they talked to each other. Instead, his father got back in the car before he'd even crossed the parking lot and entered the bus station. He started the ignition; Sam turned when he heard the car crank up and watched it glide like a steel ship across the blacktop and onto the road. He stood in front of the doors of the bus station, watching his father drive away, through one intersection and then another. All the lights were green, making haste of their parting.

There were too many people around for Sam to cry. This was his choice, and he would stick to it. He would act like a man, even though sometimes he felt like he was still a boy.

*

Dark clouds gathered in the sky as Sam sat on the hard metal bench waiting for his bus to board. He flipped through a magazine he'd found while he waited. He didn't notice the woman who sat down on the bench beside him until she spoke, her voice like a songbird.

"I can't believe you're running away."

Sam closed the magazine. He looked over to see her soft silhouette beside him. Her hair carefully pinned up into a large bun, Betty sat next to him with her legs crossed.

"How did you know I was here?" Sam hadn't told anyone he was leaving. His plan was to skip town quietly. He imagined that he wouldn't even be missed. Maybe it would be weeks before anyone realized he had gone.

"I know things about you."

"That's weird, creepy even. Is this how you try to win someone back?" He opened his magazine again and decided to read an article about making the perfect Jell-O mold.

Betty looked down at the article. She pointed at the picture of the dome of Jell-O sitting in the midst of a plate, bits of canned fruit suspended inside it as if frozen in time. "I didn't know you were interested in cooking."

Sam snapped the magazine closed. "What do you want from me?"

"Time," she said. "All I ever wanted was more time. I thought I knew how to get it, but I was wrong."

"I don't know what you're talking about." His jaw stiffened. "I'm going away to get away from you."

"I know. You're going to Boston to stay with a friend. You'll like it there. You might even stay."

Sam opened his magazine again. That time it fell open to a page about how to remove a wine stain from carpet. Sam wondered why he had picked up a women's magazine. He should've spent some money to buy something interesting that he really wanted to read.

He closed the magazine again and rolled it into a cylinder. All that time Betty sat next to him, her gaze constantly trained on him. He could feel her eyes, expectant, waiting, but he didn't know what for.

He looked up at the large clock on the wall. There were still twenty minutes before his bus would leave. The thought of spending that time with Betty sitting next to him, watching him, was almost too much to bear. He stood up and put his duffel bag over his shoulder.

She stood up too. "Where are you going?"

"To get some air." He marched outside into the heat where the air was thick with bus fumes. Betty followed close on his heels like a puppy. Several times he considered turning around and telling her to get away, but he didn't. She was as stubborn as him, and he knew that if he told her to leave, it would probably make her stay longer. Ignoring her was a tactic worth trying, but someone like that was hard to ignore.

"I'm not sure what this is accomplishing. I'm starting to sweat," Betty said.

"No one is making you stay out here. Go home."

"I know. I'm only here because I want to make sure you remember my face when you're in Boston. Don't you forget me. I'll never forget you, and you should never forget me."

"That sounds like a threat."

"It isn't meant to be. It's a tactic. It's important. I need you to see me in your dreams."

Sam already did.

He turned and walked back into the station, his shoulder growing tired from the duffel bag. Inside he set it on a bench but continued to stand up himself. Betty was still there. She wouldn't go away.

A woman's voice crackled through the speakers in the ceiling.

"My bus is boarding." Sam picked up his bag again.

"Remember me, Sam. Remember my face. Remember how it felt when we were together."

Everything she was saying was pointless because he already remembered. He always would remember. How could he not?

"I'm going."

A line of people waited to climb aboard his bus. As he stood in line, he looked straight ahead at the back of a tall, broad man in a dark gray suit who stood in front of him. Sam didn't turn around. Even though inside he wanted to take one last look, he didn't. Doing so would be like giving her something he wasn't willing to give.

"Sam!" she called out from behind him, but he wouldn't give her the satisfaction of turning around. "I'll visit you. I promise."

Sam climbed onto the bus without looking back.

Chapter Seventeen

BETTY knew she was still in the nursing home before she even opened her eyes. She heard the rattle of the cart the nurse pushed down the hallway. The nurse's rubber-soled shoes squeaked on the tile as they passed the doorway to her room. Betty reached out and felt the metal bars of the hospital bed, cold and unwelcoming against her fingers. She opened her eyes slowly, dreading seeing the room around her. It was just as she expected. She woke up in the same room she'd gone to sleep in.

Dust particles danced on the beams of morning sunlight floating through the half-open blinds. Betty shallowed hard. Her throat was cottony. She reached for the cup that sat on the table at her bedside. It was empty.

"Good morning." A nurse came in carrying a red plastic tray of food. She walked over to the small table in front of the window and placed the tray there. "Did you sleep well?"

Betty propped herself up to watch the woman. "I could use a drink. My cup is empty."

The nurse took the white Styrofoam cup from the tray and brought it over to Betty, who took two large gulps from it, nearly drinking the whole contents.

"I thought you could eat by the window today. You haven't been up recently. Do you need me to help you get up?"

Betty shook her head. "I can still take care of myself. Just put these rails down so I can get out of this bed."

The nurse released a latch on the side of the bed and the rails clattered down. "Call if you need anything," the nurse said before going back into the hall. She pushed the cart carrying the other residents' breakfasts to the next room. Betty heard her singsong voice saying, "Good morning," to the person there.

Breakfast was a bowl of lumpy cream of wheat and a few spoonfuls of canned fruit cocktail. "How much am I paying to live in this dump and eat this crap?" Betty wondered aloud as she let a lump of cream of wheat fall from her spoon and land back in the bowl with a splat. She looked out the window at the view of the beige stucco wall of another building only a few yards away. Dirt clung to the peaks in the stucco. She put her spoon down and pushed the bowl away. Though her stomach twisted with hunger, she didn't feel much like eating more than a few spoonfuls.

The antiseptic scent of cleaner hung in the air. Her room was full of sound bleeding in from the hallway, washing in from other rooms. Televisions blared. Conversations rose and fell. She listened, feeling all alone in life.

Then she noticed a familiar voice above the others. The hearty laugh bellowed. Betty got up from her chair, determined to follow the sound. Looking down, she realized she was still in her pajamas. Her yellow hair was tangled and pressed flat at the back of her head. She wasn't wearing any makeup and hadn't even put in her dentures or brushed the few teeth she still had. She thought about all these things and the effort it would take to change them for only a few seconds before grabbing her robe from the hook by the door and sliding it over her shoulders. She walked down the hallway in her stocking feet, following the voice.

The voice led her to an open door only five down from her own. The man who had been speaking was silent now. He sat in front of his window hunched over a table, shoveling hot cereal into his mouth. He wore thin blue-and-white-striped pajamas that hung loosely on his narrow shoulders. His thin gray hair stuck out in wispy flyaways.

Betty rapped on the open door to let him know she was there, and he twisted around to see her. He pulled the corners of his mouth up into a smile.

"Betty, come in." He motioned to the seat next to him. "Sit down. Join me for breakfast."

The rubber tip of Betty's cane gripped the tile floor as she made her way carefully into his room on slippery socked feet. Her hips ached, so she eased herself down into the chair, carefully positioning her cane between her knees.

The man looked at the tray in front of him, a worried expression crossing his face. "I don't have much to offer you. You can have a fruit cup. I don't like them anyway, too sweet." With a shaky hand, he picked up the plastic cup and set it in front of Betty.

"No, thank you. I have my own back in the room." In this reality where nothing was right, Betty was grateful to see a face she knew. She was even more grateful that he seemed to know her too. "You're having a good morning, Bernie."

"My mornings are usually good. It doesn't get bad till the sun goes down. That's what they tell me at least. I don't remember." He went back to eating.

"You must have been okay last night. I didn't hear anything." Betty remembered waking up in the middle of the night in a nursing home that was unusually quiet and still. She could still feel the disappointment gathering around her when she opened her eyes and realized where she was before drifting off again, before trying again to convince Sam to take her back again.

"You're too caught up in reliving your past to hear me." He winked. A white glob of hot cereal stuck to the skin just below his lower lip.

"I was, actually." Startled, Betty opened her eyes wide.

"Don't look at me like you think I can read your mind. You told me all about it. Remember?" He held his spoon perched in the air just a few inches above his bowl.

Betty shook her head.

"And they say my dementia is worse than yours." He ate the last few bites of cereal, grabbed the napkin from the tray, and quickly wiped his mouth. Somehow, he managed to miss the blob of cereal on his face.

"What did I tell you?" she asked.

He smirked. "Everything you're afraid to tell anybody else." He held both hands out. "Look at me. I'm in the same place you are. What's the harm in telling me?"

Betty knew he was right. When she first found the paper in her purse, she had told both him and Pat. Pat never mentioned it again though. Bernie, on the other hand, seemed to believe her.

"Since you're still here, I assume you haven't convinced him yet."

Betty shook her head. "No luck."

"He's moving away, then?"

Betty gave a weak smile. "I met him in the bus station last night. He didn't want to have anything to do with me."

He nodded slowly. "Have you told him about what's going on?"

"I tried, but he just thinks I'm crazy."

"That's about right. I'd think the same thing if I were him.

You have to think of another way."

Betty had been trying to think of another way for what seemed like years, but she just couldn't solve the problem. "I don't know. I woke up in this reality more than once now. I feel like this is just the way things are going to be."

"You can't control what point to go back to in your dreams?"

"No. I tried, but it didn't work. I'm not sure how all this started. I don't know how to control it." Betty would give anything to have some control over what was happening to her again. "What should I do? What should I tell him?"

"I'm no relationship expert."

"I know, but you're a man. If you were him, what would you need to hear to change your mind?"

Bernie sat back in his chair and crossed his arms over his chest. He looked up at the ceiling, his mouth clamped closed. "I don't know. I'm sorry, but I don't know."

"With the way you looked, I was sure you were going to come up with something."

He laughed. "I was hoping to pull something out of thin air, but I've never been good at that either."

Usually, she liked the sound of his laugh, but that time it felt like he was making light of all that was happening with her. "This isn't funny."

"I never said it was." He opened his mouth, taking in a gulp of air, then clamped his lips shut without saying a word.

"What?"

He shook his head.

"You were going to say something." She leaned forward in her chair, eager to hear any suggestion.

"You know how you brought that piece of paper with the phone number on it back from your dream?" He thought for a moment. "Maybe you could take something from now into your dream."

Betty shook her head. "I don't have anything to take that would prove our life together to him now. I'm not even in the reality I want to get back to anymore. Our life together only exists in my memory." Betty tapped her cane on the ground. The rhythm and the movement helped clear her mind. "Maybe the problem is that I'm always trying to tell him. Maybe I have to show him. If I show him, it should all work out just fine, right?" She looked to Bernie for any reassurance he couldn't offer.

"I'm not sure what you mean."

Betty snorted. "Neither am I, really." She ran her tongue over her lips as she thought. This wasn't an unsolvable problem. She was a smart woman. Surely, she could come up with a solution. "Bernie, you have to help me figure this out."

"Even though I've read The Time Machine three times, I'm not really an expert in time travel."

Betty whacked his arm. "You mean The Time Machine didn't have any advice about how to fix your present once you've messed around with the past?"

He rubbed the spot on his arm where she hit him. "Unfortunately, no, but it should."

"Everything about time travel should."

Chapter Eighteen

SAM loped along the city streets with his hands shoved in his pockets. He slouched, watching his shoes as he walked like he needed to see his feet to control them. The sidewalks were full of people despite the cold. Sleet had fallen the day before. Dirty slush seeped into his shoes, making the bottoms of his socks uncomfortably wet. He had spent all day in classes. Studying engineering in Boston was a great idea, but it was harder than he thought it would be.

Sam was accustomed to being the smartest in his class, but that wasn't the case here. Here he felt like his brain wasn't quite as sharp as it needed to be to compete. Everyone else knew as much as him, some more. He had never been in that situation before, and it made him uncomfortable, but he was willing to rise to the challenge.

He was thinking about class and an equation he didn't quite understand as he walked down the street. He was so busy thinking that he didn't even notice his surroundings, the people rushing past him, the cars beeping noisily on the street. Even the wind whipping through his coat went unnoticed. It was strange for a Florida boy. He should have at least noticed the cold.

He was so distracted that he didn't even realize he had a visitor until he had climbed the steps to his front door and was pulling the keys from his pocket.

"Sam," a voice said from behind him.

He knew the voice too well. Turning around, he saw Betty standing on the sidewalk in a full green skirt and black high heels. She wore no coat. Only a brown corduroy blazer covered her white sweater.

"What are you doing here?"

"I wanted to see you."

"You must be freezing." He stood holding his door open just a crack, taking her in with his eyes. She was the last person he expected to see in Boston. Her cheeks were rosy from the cold, and the end of her nose was a bit red, but she still looked more radiant than anyone he had ever seen.

"I am. Can I come inside?"

"Of course," he stammered. He returned the keys to his pocket and pushed the door wide open, gesturing for her to go inside.

She stepped into his apartment and having her there made him see his space in a new light. It was large but in disrepair. The fact that he hadn't had the chance to buy much furniture didn't help the situation. His eyes were immediately drawn to the large cardboard box he'd been using as a table. He only had one folding chair. The apartment seemed even colder than it was outside. He immediately rushed over to the thermostat on the wall to adjust the heat. The heater kicked on, giving off a burnt smell.

"Have a seat." He gestured to the single folding chair that sat in the middle of the large bare room.

He watched her eyes as she looked around, carefully examining everything, a frown carved into her face. "So, this is where you live?"

Sam immediately started stacking up the newspaper that was spread across the top of the cardboard box he used as a table. He neatly stacked it and set it on the kitchen counter. "I don't have anything to offer you to drink, just water or milk." He went into the kitchen, opened the refrigerator, and pulled out the carton of milk. He decided to give it a taste before pouring any for Betty and immediately realized it was sour. "Forget the milk, just water."

"I'm fine. Don't worry about me."

He went back into what should've been the living room, and shame gripped him as he stared at the pitiful space. The white walls were bare except for the cracks and stains left by previous tenants. A stack of books sat in the far corner of the room, and piles of papers and notepads were strewn across the floor.

His eyes landed on Betty. Noticing he was staring at her, she asked, "Are you okay?"

"Yeah." He sat cross-legged on the floor. "I'm just realizing how this must look to people, but I don't spend much time here. I'm at school a lot, and when I'm home, I'm in the bedroom."

She nodded. "I thought you were staying with a friend here."

"I was for a few days, but when this place came up, I took it because it was unbelievably cheap. If I'm going to stay, I might as well commit, right?"

Neither of them said anything for a while. They sat staring at each other. Sam had almost forgotten how beautiful she was.

"You're probably wondering what I'm doing here?"

"Yes, as a matter of fact, I am. How did you find me? Are you staying in town?"

"I don't have anywhere to stay. I only planned on being

here for a few hours." She looked around the room, concerned. "Have I taken your only chair?"

"Don't worry about it. How did you find me?"

"Your dad told me."

His father was the only person Sam kept in touch with once he left St. Pete. He had planned to start a new life with completely new friends in a completely new place. He didn't realize that wouldn't work. Even though he'd started over, his old memories haunted him. The idea of being with Betty still haunted him. He had dated several girls, but he just couldn't get her off his mind.

"You didn't come here just to see me, did you?" When he asked the question, he knew the answer he hoped to hear. Even if she was crazy and believed herself to be a time traveler, he missed her.

She nodded slowly.

Sam's heart leaped at the idea. He thought moving away would help him get over her, but it hadn't. He had dreamed about her almost every night. He wondered how she was, where she was, if she'd married Tucker. Whenever he talked to his father, he asked about Betty. His father always answered the same way, telling him that he had no idea how she was and maybe he should call her himself. He didn't. He was too proud. "Why?" he asked.

She crossed her right leg over her left and bounced her leg up and down a few quick times. Then she bit her bottom lip. She slid off the chair and onto the floor, her full skirt spreading out around her. Sam had been trying to avoid her eyes, but she wouldn't let him. She stared into his eyes long and hard, as if looking for something that was missing. Finally, she spoke.

"On August 16, 1965, our son will be born. We were trying for so long when we finally found out I was pregnant, we couldn't believe it. The delivery was hard. I wasn't in the room when you held him for the first time, but after you did, you came to the hospital room, your eyes glassy from crying, and you told me that he was beautiful and I was beautiful and we would be together forever. We never had another child. We couldn't, but Ethan was enough. Just the three of us were enough."

A tear slid down her cheek. She wiped it away with her hand. "You died before me, and as an old woman, all I do is think about what I did wrong, what I regret. The thing I regret most in life was not having more time with you. I wasted so much time with Tucker when I could've been with you. So, when all this started happening, I saw this as a perfect opportunity to go back in time and fix what I thought I had done wrong."

Sam shifted uncomfortably. He looked at the floor. He had hoped this would be a normal visit, but nothing about his conversations with Betty were normal anymore. "Stop it. What are you talking about? I really am starting to think you need to be in a mental hospital."

"I won't stop. I can't stop because you need to hear the truth. I've completely ruined our future together. Your unwillingness to believe me is making it worse. I can't have that. Our life together was the thing I cherished most. It can't be gone."

More tears fell down her cheeks. "I need you to listen to me. I need you to understand. I know this is hard for you, because you're all about facts and reason, but I need you to stop being logical and try feeling. You can do that, Sam. Try feeling. If you stop thinking about it and start feeling, you'll know I'm telling the truth."

She opened her purse and retrieved a tissue to wipe her eyes. She patted the end of her nose but didn't blow it. "You took care of your mother when she was dying. You were only thirteen, a kid. You never should've seen what you did, but your father made himself too busy at the sandwich shop when she started to get very sick. He couldn't handle it, but he should've never made you try to deal with it yourself. You would come home from school and the nurse would leave. You'd help her to the bathroom and clean up her puke. You cried every night in your room. I'm so sorry you had to go through that."

Sam had never told anyone the truth about what had happened with his mother. He always covered up how much responsibility he had to take on at such a young age because he knew it was wrong. He was angry at his father for abandoning him and his mother for the business at the time he was needed most. Sam was also embarrassed to admit to anyone what had happened. He knew it was strange, so he covered it up. When people talked about his mother and how hard it must have been for him, he never told them the whole truth.

"Who told you that?" Sam had told Betty a lot of things in the letters that he sent during the war, but he knew he didn't tell her much about his mother. He kept those memories to himself.

"You did. Just like when you told me about seeing your best friend in the war get his legs blown to smithereens. You told me you sat with him and waited for the medics to come with mortars exploding all around you. That was so brave."

Sam knew he had never told Betty about that. He had never told anyone in the world. When he was writing letters, he did his best to minimize how much danger he had been in because he didn't want her to worry. He never mentioned taking enemy fire or the injuries of his fellow soldiers, how frightening it was. He made it all sound like a vacation. "I know I didn't tell you that."

"You haven't yet, but you will."

He pushed his back into the wall. His heart raced. "Who told you that, Tucker?" It was the only thing that made sense, even though he was pretty sure Tucker didn't know either.

She blinked slowly. Her face was so calm. It didn't reflect the uneasiness bouncing around the room. "You will tell me after we're married. There will be a war in the Gulf. Everything will be so advanced that they'll show practically the whole thing live on television. I wanted to keep it on so I could see what was happening, but you didn't like it. One day you switched the TV off and you told me that story." Her lips trembled. "It's so awful. You feel like you have to keep stuff like that inside, but you don't have to keep anything from me."

Sam was aware of how quickly the air was flowing in and out of his lungs. He saw Private Riley Nelson in his mind so clearly, his leg nothing more than fragments of flesh and bone scattered in the grass. He would never forget the sight. Sam had tried not to look. Instead, he concentrated on Private Nelson's face. Nelson's expression was soft and dreamy, not the twisted agony that he associated with such an injury. He looked like he was peering into the face of an angel. Nelson talked. He talked the whole time, asking not to be left alone, but somehow, he still looked right through Sam at something Sam couldn't see. Sam was so sure Private Nelson would die that day. He was lucky he didn't.

"It's easier to go on and keep those memories inside. Outside of me, they don't do any good to anyone else in the world."

"But when you share them with me, it makes us closer." She crawled over and sat on her haunches in front of him, her face so close to his. "I want to be as close to you as possible."

Sam looked away. He couldn't stand to look directly at her.

"You should go."

She put her hand on his face and turned his head to face her. "I need you to come back home. You don't belong here. Come back to Florida with me." She leaned into him and kissed him, her mouth warm and soft and sweet. She pulled away, keeping her face close to his. "Come home."

Sam shook his head. "I started school already. I really want this."

"I understand, but you can go to school in Florida."

"You should go."

"Not until you tell me you'll think about it."

"I'll think about it."

She stood up, pulled her blazer around her torso, and turned to walk toward the door. Sam didn't get up. He sat there watching her walk away from him. She pulled the door open and, before stepping back out into the cold, said, "I love you, Sam. I will always love you."

He hadn't known that he had wanted to hear those words from her mouth again more than anything. "Goodbye, Betty."

Her face seemed to collapse, crinkling into sorrow. "Goodbye."

Chapter Nineteen

BETTTY didn't have to wake up fully to realize she was still in the nursing home. She knew when she said goodbye to Sam that he wasn't coming back. She could see it in his eyes. She knew those eyes. They'd spoken to her for so many years. She should have never left without convicting him, but her dream was coming to an end.

She opened her eyes. It was still early. The sun hadn't yet come up. Light cascaded through the crack under her door. People were talking in the hallway, their voices loud whispers, though she couldn't understand what they were saying. Betty blinked a few times. The room was not totally dark. A small dome light on the ceiling in the corner near the window let off a soft white glow, just enough to light up that corner of the room. Tears escaped her eyes, pooling on the pillow beneath her head. Her sorrow caught in her throat, and she gasped.

She lay in her bed listening to people walking up and down the hall. She could hear someone else coughing in the room next to hers. The person coughed over and over, so hard that it sounded like they might be dying. Betty wondered if someone was checking on him.

Eventually it stopped, and she drifted off to sleep again.

Chapter Twenty

SAM didn't get up to lock the door behind her after she left. He couldn't. He sat on the floor with his head in his hands, wondering how his life got to be like this.

How did she know about things he'd never told anyone? His father couldn't have told her because he didn't know about them either.

Was she telling the truth all this time? How could that be possible? It didn't make any sense, but did it really matter? When she sat on the floor in front of him, he felt something, a pinprick to his heart. His mother once told him that if he paid attention, he'd always know if someone was telling him the truth. Betty was telling the truth. He couldn't get on board with the idea that she'd traveled through time, but somehow, she knew about their future.

Even though he believed her when she told him she loved him, he'd decided to reject her because he wanted to punish her for hurting him so badly. In the process, he was only hurting himself. He couldn't let her walk away again. Not now. He had to catch her. He didn't mean to send her away.

Sam got up and darted toward the door. He opened it and looked out onto the cold city street. He had to find her.

Looking left and then right, he saw her standing on the corner wrapped in her thin jacket, puffs of condensation coming from her mouth like smoke. He started walking, but soon broke into a run. Slush splashed up around his feet. She turned and looked at him before he ever reached her, her forlorn expression brightening. He almost couldn't stop on the slick sidewalk and crashed into her. Wrapping his arms around her, he held her up.

"Does this mean I've changed your mind?" she asked.

He kissed her. She put her arms around his waist and kissed him back. The chilly air enveloped them. Their feet were cold and wet. The city buzzed around them. People brushed by in a rush to get somewhere else, but none of that mattered. At that moment in time, they were the only people in the world.

Sam pulled his face away from hers and said, "I'll go back with you, but you have to promise never to leave me again."

"I never will," she said. "I would never want to."

Chapter Twenty-One

WHEN Betty opened her eyes, everything was right. She lay in her room on her back, looking at the white stucco ceiling. She could hear Maia in the kitchen laughing and singing. Imani spoke in a steady rhythm over her sister's voice. The smell of fried potatoes and onions filled the air.

Betty got out of bed as quickly as her aching body would allow. She grabbed hold of her cane and, without even putting on her robe, hurried out to the kitchen to see if what she was hearing was true.

Ethan stood at the stove flipping potatoes in the pan. The girls sat at the table, their eyes bright, their voices rising in conversation.

Betty rushed over to her son and gave him a long hug.

"Be careful, the pan's hot." He lifted his arm and put it around her shoulder. "You're in a good mood this morning."

"I'm just so happy to see you." She turned to the girls. "And you too." She went over to them, hugging each of them as they sat in their chairs, squeezing their shoulders into her belly. Maia squirmed and laughed.

"We love you too, Grandma," Imani said.

"Where's your mother?"

"I'm right here." Tawana came into the room. "Glad to see you so happy this morning."

Betty hugged her too, and then when she suggested a big group hug, the girls were more than happy to jump from their chairs and wrap their arms around both her and Tawana.

"The potatoes will burn," Ethan said, holding a spatula in the air.

"The potatoes will survive the few seconds it will take you to come over and hug your family," Tawana said.

Ethan put the spatula down and wrapped his long arms around all of them. Betty swelled with joy at being with them again.

"Grandpa says he's glad you're back," Maia said as they let go of each other.

"Maia, stop it," Ethan said, returning to the stove.

Maia shook her head. "I can't." She looked at Betty. "He said he hopes you've learned your lesson, and he'd never change the life you've had together." She returned to her seat at the table. "That's all?" she asked the empty space in front of her. "He says he loves you. He says he loves all of us."

"Enough," Tawana scowled.

A warm feeling spread over Betty, and for a brief moment she swore she felt Sam's arms around her.

"I'm glad I'm back too," she said.

THE END

More Books by Lovelyn Bettison

SUNCOAST PARANORMAL

The Psychic
Monster in the House
Lady in the Lake
Girl in the Woods
Demon in the Mirror
Ghost in the Closet

FARRINGTON PHENOMENON

The Curse of Warner Manor
Mystery Lake

ISLE OF GODS SERIES

The Vision
The Escape
The Memory
The Revenge

<<<<>>>>